BURIED GUNS

BURIED GUNS

by

Dan Claymaker

Dales Large Print Books
Long Preston, North Yorkshire,
BD23 4ND, England.

British Library Cataloguing in Publication Data.

Claymaker, Dan
    Buried guns.

A catalogue record of this book is
available from the British Library

ISBN   978-1-84262-597-2 pbk

First published in Great Britain in 2007 by Robert Hale Limited

Copyright © Dan Claymaker 2007

Cover illustration © Gordon Crabb by arrangement with
Alison Eldred

Published in Large Print 2008 by arrangement with
Robert Hale Limited

Dales Large Print is an imprint of Library Magna Books Ltd.

Printed and bound in Great Britain by
T.J. (International) Ltd., Cornwall, PL28 8RW

This one for J.B.

CHAPTER ONE

Dusty Bing was all through with Mission Rock. The town, its mean main street, Mc-Cundrie's saloon, that sonofabitch Sheriff Prinz and his foul-smelling, louse-ridden deputies; the heat, the dust, the sand – the endless sand whichever way a fellow looked, for as far as he could see – they could all go to hell and rot there. He was out. Right now. The minute he had finished packing his few possessions and for just as long as it took to bang the door on his room at Beryl's boarding-house and saddle up that roan mare waiting on him out back. And then he would ride. Boy, would he ride! North, south, east, west ... he had no fancy. Anywhere out of Mission Rock would do. Just anywhere.

It was a further half-hour before Dusty left the room for the last time, saddled the mare, mounted up and reined the willing horse to the empty street where the thin morning light spread through a soft haze. He paused when he reached the open street and glanced to left and right. East or west, he wondered? Hell, what was the difference? Out of Mission Rock was out of Mission Rock. Who gave a cuss to where? Not him. He reined to the east and had almost urged the roan into a steady gallop when a voice halted him and he reined back sharply.

'You leavin' town, mister, or just takin' the air?' quipped Sheriff Prinz, idling against the sill of a window in the shadows of the boardwalk.

Dusty glanced along the Street again. Not a living soul in sight. How come he had missed seeing Prinz? How come the sheriff had known he was leaving? He swallowed. 'Sure,' he said nervously. 'Headin' West. Back home.'

'Then you're goin' the wrong way, fella,' Prinz grinned, settling his Winchester in the cradle of his arms. 'Way you're headin' is east.'

Dusty sweated and looked confused. 'You're right,' he groped, dropping the words like stones. 'Thanks. Should've known.'

'You should have. Got to know east from west when you hit the sand out there. It don't tell you.' The sheriff pushed himself clear of the window and strolled into the light. 'Anyhow, how come you ain't told me of your plans? You know the rules hereabouts: nobody sets foot in this town without my say; nobody leaves without it. Plain enough, fella. Everybody knows the rules.' He spat deliberately into the dirt. 'And what about your sidearm? Colt as I recall. You hand in your weapons when you arrive, collect 'em when you leave. Couldn't be clearer. How come you're ridin' gun-naked into somewhere as hostile as the sand? T'ain't a sensible thing to be doin'.'

Dusty calmed the restive mare. 'Yeah, well … o'course you're right there, Sheriff.' He worked a weak smile across suddenly parched lips. 'Kinda got a lot on my mind right now. Illness. Back home. Kin. My sister.' He licked his lips anxiously. 'Ain't expected to be of this good earth for much longer. Nossir. Sure sick she is. Desperate.'

Prinz spat again and recradled the Winchester. 'Sorry to hear that, mister. Real sorry.' He paused, raised his eyes from the already sizzling pool of spit and darkened his stare on Dusty. 'So when did you get to hear of this? I ain't had no messages through here of late. Strange I didn't get to hearin' of your dilemma.'

The roan mare snorted and tossed her

head against the tight rein. Dusty sweated, floundered, muttered something inaudible and felt his limbs begin to melt in the growing heat of the early morning. He glanced along the street again, blinked on the shimmering haze. Still nobody about. Still only silence. 'Guess–' he began.

'No matter.' The sheriff gestured, stepping forward as he dropped the rifle to a right-hand grip. 'You get movin', mister. Fast as you can. I ain't for holdin' a fella up when he's in your position. No way. If you're paid up at Beryl's all you need to do is get to ridin' west across them sands, fast as you can.' He scuffed a boot through the dirt. 'Where you headin', as a matter of interest?'

Dusty's face beaded in a fresh lathering of sweat. He tried to swallow. 'Headin'?' he croaked, his hands wet and sticky on the reins. 'Headin'...? Yeah, well, I'm headin' west. Norricott way. Sure ... Norricott.'

Prinz grimaced. 'Norricott, eh? Well, that's sure one helluva ride. You ain't goin' to make Norricott in some days. You bet. How many days you figure a ride like that will take?'

Dusty reined the mare tight again. 'I ain't rightly thought,' he floundered. 'Not close on, I ain't. Two, three, four days. Who's for reckonin'?'

'You're right, fella.' Prinz grinned. 'Who's for reckonin'? I ain't, so best thing you can do is ride. No time to collect that Colt; no time to provision up – store ain't open, anyhow – and no time to let that poor, dyin' sister of yours know you're comin'. Who cares how long it's goin' to take to reach her? What's it matter, so long as she's alive and you can say a few last words to her before she passes on. And amen to that, eh? Rest in peace. The livin' must sure as the Good Lord settles day to night and back again, honour the dyin' best they can in the time of departure. And you say a word for me, mister. Sure, you do that. Tell her as how I speeded you on your way out of Mission Rock with my full blessin'. Yessir! You bet. Now ride!'

Dusty said nothing, flickered a weak, trembling smile, loosened the reins on the restive mare and headed west down the deserted street as if blown on a freak gust of wind.

He did not look back, saw nothing of Sheriff Prinz's signal to the man on the roof of McCundrie's saloon, the gleam of the rifle barrel as it steadied in its aim. And he certainly never heard the two fast shots that blew a hole in his back.

Dusty was dead before he hit the dirt, where his blood congealed in seconds in the deepening heat. The roan mare galloped on, gathering pace in her freedom, heading due west.

Deep in the shadows of the boardwalk fronting Wickham's mercantile and town store, Doc Cherry watched as Sheriff Prinz shouldered his rifle, waved his approval to the marksman on the roof and lit a celebratory cigar.

Doc grunted quietly to himself, picked up his medicine-bag and stepped into the sunlight to confirm Mission Rock's twentieth killing.

CHAPTER TWO

The morning haze had cleared and the heat through Mission Rock had thickened by the time Doc Cherry was all through with the preparations for the burial of Dusty Bing, and town undertaker, Elmer Puce, was busying himself with the familiar practicalities.

'Poor devil had no kin as I heard tell. Just

a loner. Drifted in and out from nowhere,' Elmer had reflected as he measured the body for its coffin. 'He ain't goin' to be missed by my reckonin'. You want me to say some words over him when I'm ready, Doc?'

'If you wouldn't mind' said Doc, gazing into the street from the funeral parlour's window. 'I'll be with that so-called sheriff of ours, and this time I want some explanations. Proper explanations. Explanations that make sense and are the law, not some trumped up version that suits Prinz's books.' He sighed and gripped the lapels of his coat. 'Time's come, Elmer. Town can't go on like this.'

'You're plumb right there, Doc,' said Elmer, licking the tip of his pencil as he made another note on his pad. 'There ain't a livin' soul here as ain't scared through to his pants – beggin' the ladies' pardon – scared rotten at what's happened and what's continuin' to happen. Damnit, the way Prinz and his gunslingin' sidekicks have got this town sewn up a fella feels as if he's a prisoner in his own home.' Elmer grunted and licked the pencil again. 'Can't come or go without Prinz's say-so. Can't do nothin' without Prinz's say-so. Know somethin'? I bet that murderin' swine keeps a check on

15

when a fella takes a wash!'

Doc turned from the window and held up a hand to soothe Elmer's growing temper.

'I hear you, Elmer, I hear you. What you're sayin' is what we all feel, but all the shootin' in the world, all the words you can mouth, ain't goin' to change Prinz or get rid of his sidekicks. No, shoutin' ain't the way, same as tryin' to get guns for some shoot-out – even if we were armed – would never work, save create a bloodbath the likes of which ain't never been seen. There's got to be another way. There's got to be a reason for Prinz holdin' the town hostage these past twelve months. There has to be an answer, somewhere, somehow... But as yet I ain't got a clue to it.'

Doc sighed deeply, adjusted his hat and collected his bag. 'I'm all through here, Elmer. I'll leave it to you.'

'Sure, Doc, you leave it to me. Fact, I'm gettin' lucky here – Dusty is a standard size. Got a box ready and waitin'. Save on the timber. All ready for the next time.'

Doc left and walked slowly through the shadows in the direction of Sheriff Prinz's office. The next time, he pondered, recalling Elmer's words, the next time...

That was the trouble, there would be a

next time.

The cigar-smoke curled like dull breath through the open door and window of Sheriff Prinz's office. Just as it always did after a killing.

Inside, Prinz and his sidekick deputies, Mouthy Kline, Skeets Murphy and Chine Billet, would be toasting their success in once again containing the townsfolk, maintaining their interpretation of the law and strengthening their grip of fear. 'Town's ours, boys, and that's the way it's goin' to stay,' Prinz would say with a smile, raising his glass to the lounging men. 'And one day soon the rewards will be ours to share.'

Mouthy Kline would sneer and dribble through his twisted lips. Skeets Murphy would fidget, finger the butt of his Colt and wonder how much longer he had to wait before Ma McCundrie opened the saloon and let loose the bar-girls. Chine Billet would only grunt, finish his whiskey in a single gulp and belch loudly on a rumbling gut.

'And that miserly little weasel Dusty Bing never knew a thing,' Prinz was saying as Doc Cherry approached along the board-walk. 'Nice shootin', Chine! Real professional.'

'I *am* professional,' quipped Billet. 'I've always been professional. Ain't none better, not no place.'

'Sure,' counselled Prinz, refilling his glass from an already half-empty bottle. He examined the glowing tip of his cigar for a moment, closed his eyes on some private thought, and opened them again to the sight of Doc darkening the doorway.

'Ah, mornin', Doc,' the sheriff grinned. 'You finished out there? All in order?'

'Dusty Bing is dead, shot in the back if that's what you're waitin' to hear,' said Doc, suppressing a surge of anger as the sweat beaded freely across his brow.

'He knew the rules.' Prinz frowned. 'He didn't obey them – and there's a price to be paid if you don't obey. A very high price.' The frown lightened. 'Damnit, you know the situation, Doc. You ain't no fool.'

'Would it have made the slightest difference if Dusty had said as how he was leavin' town and asked for the return of his Colt?'

Prinz stared long and deep into Doc's eyes. 'Don't know what you're sayin' there, Doc, but Dusty Bing was lyin'. He no more had a sister out West, let alone a dyin' sister, than I've got an elephant stabled out back. He lied. He cheated. He didn't obey. And he paid the price. Them's the facts.'

'Facts as you fashion 'em, Prinz, in a long line of deaths: blatant, cold-blooded shootin's for no good reason save those you concoct to suit your needs, whatever they may be, in God's name.'

Doc swallowed. Prinz stared, fingering his empty glass across the top of his desk. Kline dribbled. Murphy bit a lip with impatience. Billet's gut rumbled into silence.

'Town and its folk have law and they have order,' said Prinz slowly, still staring. 'It's a safe place, guaranteed by me and my men. Sure, we have rules. What decent-livin' town don't? Rules make the order, build the safety. Who needs freedom to come and go when all there is out there in them damned sands is murder, mayhem, rape and pillage? I guard against that. We don't hold to no such thing here – so we don't need guns, do we, savin' mine and those of the boys there? What is a fella goin' to do with a gun 'ceptin' set about scarin' the cotton socks off folk? No, Doc, we've got it right. Mission Rock is safe and in my care. Folk should be grateful for that. Real grateful.'

Doc swallowed. He was hearing the same argument, the same spiel, delivered in almost the same words. He was conscious of

Kline tittering; Murphy strolling to the window, his gaze narrowed on the saloon bar's batwings; of Billet selecting a Winchester, a cloth, and beginning to polish the barrel.

Prinz came to his feet, joined Doc at the door and led him to the sidewalk. 'Thanks for your services this mornin', Doc,' he said quietly. 'Put it on the bill. Meantime, give yourself a break, get yourself to McCundrie's there and tell Ma you're to help yourself – Elmer too – from my personal bottle.'

'I don't think so,' murmured Doc, stepping into the dusty street. 'I'll just go clean up before the next killin'.'

Prinz stared, frowned, then spat into the dirt as he watched Doc make his slow way down the street. The fellow was becoming irritating, he pondered, scratching the dark stubble on his chin; too damned curious, too likely to step clear of the rules, and a whole sight too damned ready to question them. One of these days he might go too far. He might be trouble.

He beckoned Kline to him. 'Keep a close eye on him, will you? Him and that undertaker. I don't want them meddlin' where it ain't wanted. You get me?'

'Got it boss,' dribbled Mouthy. 'You want I should–'

'No, Doc's too useful at the moment. I still need him. Takin' him out can come later when we're all good and ready – more particularly when Mitchell and his boys make their move out Northforks way. Meantime, Skeets and Chine will seal the town tighter. That Doc might get to stirrin' some trouble. We stifle it now, but go easy. Nothin' too hard.' He grinned and slapped Kline across the back. 'Mission Rock's a nice peaceful place, ain't it? Peaceful and law-abidin'...'

CHAPTER THREE

Ten miles west of Mission Rock where the main trail settled to a shimmering sprawl of rock and sand and the air thickened in the unremitting daytime heat, a tall man astride a grey mount watched through dark narrowed eyes as the saddled riderless horse made its slow, near exhausted way towards him.

He had been following the horse's progress since first seeing it through the early-morning light as little more than an approaching swirl of dust in an otherwise barren landscape. Now, he was intrigued. Where was the rider? What had happened to him? Had he fallen sick some place way back, or maybe been attacked by bushwhacking drifters? Where had the fellow come from; where had he been heading?

Bushwhackers would have kept the horse. It had a value. No man with a grain of sense would abandon his mount in country like this; no man would be careless enough or dumb enough to lose it. But if the fellow had been shot and the horse spooked into a wild dash into nowhere...

The watching man rubbed the grey mount's ears then patted its neck. 'Best go take a look,' he murmured, adjusting his broad-brimmed hat to deepen the shade over his tanned mahogany features.

He urged the mount from the shadows of the outcrop of boulders into the glare and joined the trail at a steady, unhurried pace. He was in no sweat to be any place, not now he was within an hour or so of his objective. And the roan mare out there was in need of his help.

Twenty minutes later he was soothing the horse's mouth with a water-sodden rag.

Doc Cherry had progressed no further than

the shaded boardwalk fronting the saloon when the creak and squeak of Ma McCundrie's wicker wheelchair drew his attention and halted him.

Ma's flat, fleshy hands, the finger muscles bulging with the effort of propelling the proprietor's heavy, black-skirted, high-buttoned bulk through the wings, worked the chair to the deepest shade and came to a rest. She removed the freshly lit cheroot from the corner of her mouth, turned her staring gaze on Doc from beneath a thatch of tightly bunned hair, and grunted.

'Poor devil never stood a chance,' she said bluntly, her voice grating through years of saloon-bar smoke and booze. 'Shot him in the back. Saw it all through that window back of me.' She inhaled deeply on the cheroot, blew the smoke to the veranda ceiling and leaned forward. 'You seen Prinz?' she asked. 'What excuse this time?'

'Same as usual,' said Doc, stepping to the shade to mop his brow against the thickening heat. 'Dusty broke the rules.'

Ma slapped her hands on the wheelchair's arms, her bulk shifting against the creaking wicker. 'Rules my backside!' she scoffed before spitting clear of the shade to the dirt. 'That was murder in anybody's book, mister. Murder all through. Damn it, I seen it, same as I've seen most of the others since Prinz pinned that badge on himself. And don't you fret, Doc, I'll be tellin' him just that to his face. You bet!' She spat again.

'Won't make a blind bit of difference,' said Doc, still mopping his brow. 'You know Prinz well enough, Ma. He won't change none till whatever he's doin' is done. And Lord above knows when that'll be.'

'Sonofa-goddamn-bitch, if I weren't battened down like I am, I'd be at that Prinz like a–'

'And dead before you could blink. Prinz and them sidekicks are ruthless. They kill to survive at any price, and they ain't one bit fussed who they're murderin' or why.' Doc mopped the brim of his hat and replaced it. 'Take my advice, Ma, stay clear of trouble. I've had enough of dead bodies. Don't want to see any more – but I will, I will... That's written large as life itself.'

Ma cursed under her breath. 'I hear you well enough, Doc, but goddamnit, it sure as hell riles some to think of my place here turned into little more than a cathouse for murderin' scumbags. After all these years ... all this work and scrapin' and savin' and doin' my darndest...' She drew on the cheroot again, blew the smoke in a cloud and hid behind it. Maybe to hide a quiet tear, wondered Doc?

'Take heart, Ma,' he murmured quietly, tempted to come to her side, but thinking better of it. Ma was not much for demonstrations of compassion. 'You never know,' he added, 'somethin' might turn up.'

'Yeah,' said Ma, 'and I might grow new legs overnight! Meantime,' she went on between more clouds of smoke, 'Shamrock wants to see you, right now, if you've the time. She says it's important.'

Doc frowned, shrugged, picked up his bag and stepped to the boardwalk. 'Lovely lady like Shamrock ain't for bein' kept waitin', I guess.' He smiled.

'Get in there, you old devil!' Ma grinned as Doc pushed open the batwings.

There was a close, anxious silence through the dimly lit and deserted bar, broken only by the shadowy figure of Mopps, the pot-man and cleaner, and the slow swish of his unhurried besom. Doc paused only to nod his good morning and proceed quietly up the stairs to the first floor balcony where Shamrock's room overlooked the Street.

Shamrock had been the leading bar-girl

and Ma McCundrie's right hand, so to speak, for close on ten years. She ruled her flock of half-dozen girls with a firm but fair hand, and treated customers with a no-nonsense approach. 'Play rough with my gals, you play rough with me,' was Shamrock's ruling. And no man with a brain between his ears, crossed her. Ever.

But she had grown increasingly uncertain, and sometimes downright nervous, since the arrival of Prinz. He and his boys were not welcome, but had to be tolerated under threat of disfiguration and worse, particularly in the case of Skeets Murphy, who divided his life in equal parts between shooting men in cold blood and taking Shamrock's girls for free.

On this morning, however, and in spite of the usual rough night at the hands of Prinz, there was a glow and a freshness about her as she opened the door to Doc's tap and ushered him into her room.

'Good news, Doc,' she said, putting the finishing touches to the making of her bed. She turned, folded her arms across her breasts and smiled with a warmth Doc had not seen in months.

'Oh,' he said, easing his bag to the floor, then removing his hat, 'and what might that be? Whatever, it sure looks to have done you a power of good.'

'You bet it has!' The smile widened, her eyes sparkled. 'Guess what?'

'I can't and I wouldn't, not in a million years. Tell me.'

Shamrock unfolded her arms, smoothed the already immaculate folds of her dress, and said,

'I, Doc, have got a gun – in fact, I've got more than one – I've got five. How about that? Five! And there's more to come.'

Doc's brow beaded in a new coating of sweat, while at the same time a cold chill skidded down his spine. 'But how?' he croaked at last, fumbling for his bandanna. 'I mean, how and from where in heaven's name? It ain't possible to lay a hand on a gun in this town without Prinz's say-so, and then only for as long as it takes him or one of his rats to shoot you in the back. So how come–'

'Mebbe you'd best not ask,' said Shamrock with a flutter of her eyelids that ended in a wink. 'You wouldn't really want to know.'

'But I *am* askin' and I do want to know,' spluttered Doc, mopping his brow. 'Hell, Shamrock, if what you're tellin' me is for real, then you, my gal, are a livin' keg of dynamite. But not for long, once Prinz gets to hear.'

Shamrock turned to her dressing-table, opened a drawer and took out a bottle of Ma's quality whiskey. She poured two measures into glasses, offered one to Doc and raised her own.

'I know it's early,' she said quietly, a calmness settling across her face, 'but I believe that for the first time in months we can see a chink of light in a way to finishin' Prinz and gettin' our town back to where it belongs, so let's drink a toast, Doc – to our future.'

Shamrock sank her drink in a single gulp, waited for Doc to sip nervously at his own, then patted the bed for him to sit at her side.

'Relax and listen to what I'm goin' to tell you...'

CHAPTER FOUR

'Sorry, I don't apologize one bit for what I've done, and no, damn it, what I'm goin' to keep doin' 'til we're all through with this once and for all. And that's the truth of it,

Doc. I think – no, I believe, I'm doin' right. No regrets.'

Shamrock stretched back to the bottle of whiskey on her dressing-table, replenished Doc's glass and refilled her own. 'What d'you reckon?' she asked, almost nervously.

'Reckon?' croaked Doc, looking deep into the glass in his hand. 'I'll tell you just what I reckon, young lady: I reckon you're mad, clean out of your mind, just about the most irresponsible, ridiculous female I've ever come across in all my born days – but, hell, you are just somebody, and that's no mistake!' He placed the glass on the floor, sighed and planted a kiss full on Shamrock's lips. 'And if I were thirty years younger ... yeah, well, that don't get to thinkin' to.'

'If you were thirty years younger, Doc, we'd both be figurin' it didn't bear thinkin' to!' smiled Shamrock. 'But for now, tell me, will it work? Have we got a chance, just a glimmer of hope, or am I thrown' myself to the dogs for nothin'? Just tell me.'

Doc collected his glass, stared into it, finished the measure in one gulp, and said, 'Know somethin', it might, it just damn well might, but only if we think this through real careful from here on. Step by careful step. There ain't no other way.'

Shamrock sighed, tossed her loose hair and gazed at Doc with wide, round eyes that gleamed even in the shadowy gloom of the room. 'I've been prayin' you'd say that; prayin' day-long that the only man I trust here would say just what you've said. So now what? Where do we go from here?'

'Hold on, I've got some thinkin' to do.' Doc came thoughtfully to his feet, walked to the window, stared into the street, and began:

'Let me get this full clear. Supplies into Mission Rock are delivered once monthly out of Norricott. That includes orders for the mercantile, the livery and Ma McCundrie's saloon. And that's been a pattern for ... hell, long as I can remember. 'Ceptin' now, of course, deliveries are controlled by Prinz who knows exactly what comes in, what goes out. No messin'. Correct?'

'Correct,' said Shamrock.

Doc turned from the window. 'A long-standin' part of this pattern has been Ma's hospitality to the wagon men makin' those deliveries. She offers ... well, whatever is needed or, within reason, asked for. Again, supervised mainly by Prinz and his boys, the wagon men at this point bein' disarmed – as is Prinz's town rule – until they leave. Prinz feels safe, the wagon men ain't fussed none and stay happy. They're only doin' a job. But you, my dear, spotted a gap in the routine – that so?'

Shamrock's face brightened with a broad smile. 'You bet. The wagon team has been the same for years. Same faces, same behaviour, same everythin' about them until a coupla months back. And then it changed. A new face appeared on the scene. A younger fella by the name of Denes.'

'So tell me again, in your own words, what happened?'

Shamrock closed her eyes, opened them again, got up from the bed, walked slowly round the room for a moment, before joining Doc at the window where they both stared into the hot, deserted street where even the flies had buzzed into shade.

'This is the bit that don't come easy,' said Shamrock, closing her eyes again as her hands slid down her thighs. 'Still,' she brightened suddenly with a smile, 'it's what we're winnin' that's the important thing.'

Doc placed an arm across her shoulders. 'You bet.'

'Didn't have to be no genius to figure the score with young Denes minute I clapped eyes on him. He had that look. God, I've seen it a thousand times and thought by now I'd put it behind me. Like Ma says, I supervise; we all share the profit. And I'm good at supervisin'!'

'You don't have to tell me.' Doc smiled.

'Denes was no different from others long-since forgotten, but he persisted; it was goin' to be me or no one.' Shamrock took a long breath, looked at the bottle of whiskey, but resisted the temptation. 'For the sake of peace around the place and those damned supplies which Prinz would have stopped just like that, had he mind to, I reckoned I was goin' to have to do whatever Denes...'

Shamrock reached hurriedly for the bottle, gulped a measure fast as she could, closed her eyes and murmured. 'He was little short of an animal.'

'No need for the detail, my dear,' said Doc, 'just your thoughts and what happened so's I've got it clear.'

'I came to reckonin' it fast,' continued Shamrock, replacing the bottle on the dressing-table. She flicked at her hair, stared into the street, and went on, 'Denes weren't exactly cash-happy. Third hand on a supplies wagon don't make a fellow rich, and he would certainly never have been able to pay my price. But mebbe there was another way.

Supposin', I figured, I asked for payment in kind: guns. He had access to 'em back in Norricott; I had the means of payin' for them – with interest – and he, once the plans were set and workin', would be beholden to me, and my favours.' Shamrock shivered and tried to snuggle into her dress. 'In other words, Doc, I was payin' *him* to abuse *me* in return for five guns a delivery, hidden in a barrel which only myself, Denes, Ma and Mopps know about, and now yourself.'

Doc turned away from the window. 'You say there's more to come?'

'Five. Next delivery.'

'And where precisely are you hidin' these guns?'

'Mopps knows this saloon better than most. There's an old cellar, never used, and that's where they are, wrapped in oil-cloth. The next delivery will join 'em soon as the barrels are into Ma's cellar.'

Doc grunted. 'And when is the next delivery?'

'Two days from now – but this time there's a difference.'

Doc's eyes narrowed as he gazed into Shamrock's slowly weakening glow.

She pulled herself together with stiffening shoulders, and said, 'I've paid a high price,

Doc, the highest I've ever paid or ever will again, but this time there's goin' to be fifteen in the barrel. Is that goin' to be enough, twenty in all? For God's sake, tell me it is.

And then she began to brush away the tears.

CHAPTER FIVE

It was a full two hours later that the second shooting of that day took place in Mission Rock's main street.

The heat had deepened to an almost unbreathable air that left a heat haze shimmering no matter where a fellow turned his gaze; and the shade was no easier. But for Franky Scripps, the day was much the same as any other; an early visit to Ma McCundrie's just as soon as the bar was open, a steady intake of whiskey until around noon when, pretty well without a care in the world, he would make his slow, uncertain way back to the shack he had long since occupied at the back of Tinker Johnny's boots emporium, there to sleep it off until it was time to scrape together a few more dollars for the evening session. There was nothing complicated, threatening, even noticeable about Franky's pattern of behaviour. He was just a simple fellow with simple needs in a simple existence.

On this day, however, he ran foul of Skeets Murphy, or rather crossed his path at a time when Murphy was feeling particularly aggrieved on account of how Ma had insisted that today the bar-girls would not be available for business until mid-afternoon.

'Goddamnit, fella,' she had ranted, spinning the wicker wheelchair through a full, creaking circle, 'them gals is human same as you and me – though in your case, I ain't so sure. They'll be here when Shamrock says and I'm good and ready. Meantime, I suggest you get back to whatever no-good duty that monkey of a sheriff has ordered and simmer down some. You look like a kid who's just had his candy-bar whipped from him!'

Ma had neither regard nor respect for Prinz and his gun-happy sidekicks and had shamelessly used the confines of her wicker prison to curse them as she saw fit and the mood took her, safe in the belief that no scum, not even Prinz's men, would sink so low as to abuse an afflicted old lady. She also controlled the saloon, ran it like a liverish school ma'am and, which was more important to Murphy, ultimately controlled the girls. It was the girls who always bothered Murphy and honed his darker side to a bad edge.

Thus it was that, angered by Ma and her stubborn ruling, and fired up with a bellyful of early-morning booze, he met Franky Scripps making his unsteady way back to his shack.

'Know somethin',' Murphy had sneered, barring Franky's way down the boardwalk, 'you're a disgrace to the town. You hear that – I said a disgrace.'

Franky had said nothing, being still sober enough to realize that silence was the only defence when Murphy was in this mood.

'If I had my way, I'd rid this town of folk like you. Sure I would. Shoot 'em where they stood.' He spat. 'You ain't no better than a louse-ridden rat.'

Franky had attempted to pass Murphy, only to have his way barred by the man's threatening bulk.

'You wanna pass me, fella,' Murphy had said with a grin, the sweat gleaming on his unshaven face, 'you ask real polite.'

Franky had only gazed, first into Murphy's eyes, then round the street as if seeking support. There was no one. Not a face at a window, not a shadow in a doorway.

'Well,' said Murphy, 'you goin' to ask or just stand there like the heap of trash you are?'

Franky had made another move to pass, but in trying stumbled, lost what little balance he had and pitched headlong into Murphy.

It took only five seconds for Murphy to curse, Franky to stammer an audible apology and for Murphy to then draw his Colt and shoot Franky clean through the heart.

One shot. A second followed as the sniggering deputy stepped over the dead body and went on his way down the boardwalk, the Colt still smoking in his hand.

There was a tense, close silence in the dimly lit barn back of George Wickham's store that night as the town men gathered soon after dark.

The meeting had been called and news of it passed on, mouth to whispering mouth, among those who met regularly to discuss town matters, by Tinker Johnny.

'I'm tellin' you, I seen it all. Right there,

outside the store. Plumb on. No mistakin'. That scumbag Murphy shot Franky Scripps point blank. And him not armed. Not so much as a twist of string. Murder. Ain't no other way to sayin' it. And, hell, I'm sayin' it!'

The meeting had lapsed to a familiar silence at Tinker's outburst. What was there to say? Nobody doubted Tinker's word. He had been there, seen it first hand. Trouble was, nobody had an answer. All the anger, the disgust, the sheer hatred had been voiced before, many times. And so Elmer Puce had measured and prepared yet another body for Boot Hill.

But two in one day was different. Very different.

'Say what you like, any which way you put it,' said an old man at last, stuffing the butt end of a smoked cigar into his pipe, 'we need a miracle here. Big as they come. Big as that Good Lord up there can make it.'

The old man lit the pipe to the murmurings of the meeting.

'He's right – damned right!' cursed a man.

'Ain't nothin' else for it way I see it,' agreed another.

'So who's got a miracle goin'?' asked a grinning youth, swigging swiftly on a bottle. 'Can we buy one? Send for one? Get the

magic-man and pull it out of a hat? Bah!'
He grinned some more, taking another
swig. 'Give me a gun, any gun, I ain't fussed,
and I'll do it for you. Right now. Tonight. I'll
have Prinz and them scum–'

'Sure, sure,' soothed Doc Cherry, entering
the barn without a sound and closing the
door quietly behind him. 'No question of it,
son. You'd do it, or at least try.' The dim
lantern-light lit the soft blue of his old eyes.
'But I'd be noddin' to Elmer here to measure up them pine planks he's got stacked
out at his place faster than a fella my age can
spit.' He smiled softly. 'No, son, findin' you
a gun – even if we could – ain't goin' to be
no miracle. But thanks for the offer. It's
appreciated.'

'So what is the answer?' asked Picky
Layton, the town barber, smoothing his
already oiled hair. 'You got one, Doc?'

'It's a fair question,' said George Wickham, the store-owner. 'We've sure as hell
asked it often enough and got nowhere.
Shootin's keep happenin'; bodies pile up.
Don't appear to be no end to it. So where we
headin' in all this? Prinz and his boys just go
on and on and on... No rhyme nor reason,
just sheer bloody–'

'I see all that, George,' said Doc. ''Course,

39

I do, and mebbe there is a way, or leastways *might* be a way. But it's goin' to take time...' Doc faltered, regretting that he might be at a point of revealing Shamrock's plan. 'I say might,' he recovered hurriedly, 'and that's only a–'

'Hell, Doc,' called a man perched on a hay-bale at the back of the barn, 'you're flounderin' like the rest of us.'

The gathering nodded and murmured its agreement.

'When ain't we flounderin'?' called the grinning youth behind another swig from the bottle. 'It's like I just said, give me a gun, any gun, and I'll–'

'Will you cut the gun talk, boy,' snapped Wickham. 'That ain't no answer, not now it ain't. But meantime, I've been reckonin'...' The store-owner crossed through the low glow of the lantern, stopped, raised his eyes to the cobwebbed rafters, turned again and addressed the watching men. 'Somebody, somehow, has got to get out of town and raise help. Now, I ain't sayin' exactly how it's goin' to be done, but supposin'–'

'Ain't a horse to be had,' said Hank Stone, the blacksmith. 'My livery ain't had a horse to beg, borrow, or buy in months. There just ain't one, save on Prinz's agreement. So you can f'get it.'

'I know, I know,' said the storeman, beginning to pace. 'I've thought of that. But...' he turned sharply, 'but there is a wagon. The supplies wagon. Prinz lets that in, and it's due again in two days. Now, if we could somehow smuggle a man aboard that–'

'Hang on there, George,' clipped Tinker Johnny, 'that wagon team ain't goin' to go along with that. If they got caught... If Prinz found out... Hell! They'd be dead men!'

'But they might agree – for a price,' said Wickham, with a wink as he tapped the side of his nose. 'At a price, eh, gentlemen? They say every man has his price.'

'You talkin' bribery here, George?' said Tinker slowly, his eyes narrowing, brow furrowing. 'An out-and-out bribe? Money? Supplies? What, f'cris'sake? How do you reckon it?'

The gathering in the barn had fallen into a stiff silence. Even the youth had lost interest in the bottle. The old man's pipe lay tight between his teeth, the thin, wispy smoke drifting like a shredded ghost across the lantern-glow.

Doc shifted uneasily. Any suggestion of the town men negotiating a deal with the wagon team, and particularly Denes, would be sure to undermine Shamrock's plan, if not expose it. And then, God alone knew what the consequences might be. But dare he confide the plan to the men gathered here? Was this the time, the place? Who was to be trusted?

He glanced quickly over the faces fixed on George Wickham, tense and waiting for him to continue.

'Call it what the hell you will – bribery if you like – but gettin' somebody hidden aboard that wagon, unknown to Prinz and his men, somebody not likely to be missed; somebody on his way to get help … and then, gentlemen, we are gettin' somewhere.' Wickham smiled, his face gleaming in the soft light. 'And a man called Denes, one of the wagon team, is just the man to approach.'

Doc was about to interrupt when the barn door creaked open and a small boy, no more than five or six, peered wide-eyed into the gloom, and spluttered nervously, 'Ma says as how somebody should come real quick and see what's just fetched up outside Sheriff Prinz's office. Dusty Bing's horse!'

CHAPTER SIX

The main street was more crowded and alive that night than it had been for weeks. Doc Cherry and the storekeeper had led the town men from the barn to the pool of yellow light spreading from the windows of Prinz's office within minutes of hearing the boy's message.

'And just how the hell did that get there?' the old-timer had shouted above the sudden babble of voices.

'Let's go see for ourselves,' Tinker Johnny had urged.

'Goddamnit, if there ain't no rest to be had in this town save that on Boot Hill – God rest their sleepin' souls,' grumbled the undertaker, licking the tip of his pencil out of habit.

'Boy says that mount of Dusty's is all tacked and saddled up, just as it was when the poor devil rode out this mornin',' said Hank Stone, keeping pace alongside Doc and Wickham. 'Some horse, eh?'

'You should know, Hank,' muttered Wickham, pulling at his sweat-filled collar. 'You saw to it.'

The crowd of men halted and waited in a silent gathering outside Prinz's office, all eyes fixed on the saddled mount hitched to the rail.

'Didn't hitch itself, did it?' murmured a man at Doc's shoulder. 'I ain't never known that.'

'Me neither,' agreed a man behind him, 'and I've seen some smart horses.'

'Been trailed in – or ridden – one or the other,' said Picky Layton. 'You reckon, Hank?'

But the blacksmith swallowed his words as the office door opened, a brighter shaft of light hit the boardwalk and Prinz filled the space, his bulk silhouetted to the deepest black in which there was only the gleam of eyes and the glint of a rifle barrel.

'Seen enough?' he boomed, his voice grating through cigar-smoke and whiskey. 'Dusty Bing's horse in case anyone ain't yet recognized it.'

'Yeah,' piped the old-timer, releasing a mass of smoke from his pipe, 'and it didn't get here by itself, did it? You bet to it.'

Prinz's deputies sauntered onto the board-walk like bodies released from the underside of a stone. The sheriff gripped his rifle. The crowd muttered among themselves. Doc caught a glimpse of Shamrock ushering her girls back to the bar. Wickham cleared his throat. Pinky Layton sweated. The youth with the bottle finished the dregs. The black-smith stared at the mount as if dissecting it. The boy who had delivered the message edged to his mother's side and clung to her skirts.

'You got any reckonin' on this, Sheriff?' asked the old-timer, grinning behind another cloud of thickening smoke. 'Sure beats me.'

Prinz glared, his eyes skimming like shooting-stars over the town men's half-shadowed faces. He gripped the rifle a shade tighter. His sidekicks stood motionless. The silence deepened until even the scuff of a boot through sand seemed like a thud. Everyone sweated.

'Sure I've got a reckonin' on it,' said Prinz at last. 'Simple enough. Somebody found the poor creature out there in the desert and brought him in, didn't he? That don't take no reckonin'. Some fella watered him and then hitched him right here front of my office. And a mighty kindly gesture at that. Real decent. Deserves a reward.' He paused to spit almost deafeningly into the dirt. 'Anyone of you worthy citizens responsible? 'Cus if you are, you step up right now and let me shake you by the hand. Yessir!'

Not a voice was raised. Not a body moved. The old man's pipe-smoke curled and drifted. The youth held the empty bottle almost without a grip. Doc seethed quietly, glancing anxiously to the saloon where Shamrock and Ma McCundrie watched from the shadowed boardwalk. The store-owner simply sweated.

'So what happened to this carin' fella?' called a voice from somewhere in the shadows. 'Why ain't he here now? Why didn't he stop to explain?'

'He just some good horse Samaritan, Sheriff?' echoed another to a background of murmurings. 'Does he just happen to hang around out there in that damned bakin' sand on the look-out for stray horses? I ain't heard of nobody of that callin' before!'

A few of the men began to titter behind hands raised carefully to their mouths. Ma McCundrie creaked her wicker wheelchair and shouted, 'Tell us, Mr Prinz, seein' as how you've had a reckonin' on the situation. We want to know!'

Prinz stiffened, the sweat beading heavily

on his face. The sidekicks watched him, waiting for an order.

The old man's face and head were lost in a swirl of pipe-smoke. The youth dropped the bottle to the dirt. Hank Stone leaned forward to get a still closer look at the hitched mount.

Prinz smiled, easing the Winchester to a one-handed grip at his side. He glanced at the deputies. 'Don't get smart, fellas. It just don't pay – not in this town it don't.'

A volley of fire from the three sidekicks aimed high above the heads of the town men ripped into the silence like splinters of lightning.

'Enough,' boomed Prinz through the fading echoes of the shots. 'Clear the street right now. Every last man of you. I don't want to hear another word, not from no-body.' He gestured with the rifle. 'You hear me – clear the street before I get to doin' it myself!'

'He's mad,' said a man, risking the flame from a match to light a half-smoked cheroot.

'He ain't sane, that's for sure,' agreed the fellow at his side, closing his eyes as he inhaled the slow drift of the smoke.

'Or mebbe he ain't so crazed as you can

get to believin',' began a man sat alone in the shadows at the back of Wickham's barn. 'Mebbe he's hidin' somethin'. Damnit, he must have known that nobody was takin' in all that fancy talk about a good Samaritan sittin' out there in the sands watchin' for stray horses. No way. And specially when they're all saddled up same as Dusty's was. Hell, who's the fool in that?'

The few town men who had cleared the street on Prinz's orders and gathered in the barn, murmured, muttered, scuffed boots and hung their heads. The drinking youth, who had acquired a fresh bottle of booze, swigged it carelessly and dribbled dregs down his chin. A loose, fearful dog had wandered to the old man's side, licked his hand and welcomed the love of a scratch behind its left ear.

'Now don't let's get to speculatin' and goin' where we ain't got a clue,' said Doc Cherry, raising his arms for calm as he stepped into the glow from the lantern. 'Prinz ain't of a mind such as we know it, and that's for sure, and my considered medical opinion. But that ain't to say he's mad. There's one helluva fine line between–'

'Goddamnit, Doc,' groaned a man, hooking thick, calloused hands into his braces, 'we ain't in your mornin' surgery! We're right here and we're real spooked, right through. We ain't got no place to go. What we need is a prospect of a future and a plan to get us there – real fast. Figure that!'

The town men nodded; the youth swigged; the old man drew the dog to him, grabbed it and hugged it lovingly to his chest.

'I will,' said Doc above the hum of murmurings and muttered agreement. 'I will, I promise you. And by this time tomorrow, right here. You got my word on it!'

Doc glanced round him, shook the hands extended to his; sweated, smiled and wondered why in God's name, he was off his head.

The lantern-glow died and the men shuffled silently into the heat-drenched night.

CHAPTER SEVEN

'But that's the whole trouble, ain't it? I can't see no way of keepin' that promise I've just made to the town men of comin' up with somethin' for folk to cling to. I was frenzy-

49

headed to even think it. Just darned stupid!'

'Easy there, easy.' Shamrock smiled, patting the bed in her softly lit room above the bar as she urged Doc to sit beside her. 'Never mind that. Let's figure what's happened tonight. What've we got? A full-saddled, perfectly healthy horse – looked to, tended and watered – when it should have been dead out there in the sands long back. So ... who did the tendin', the waterin' and, more to the nub of it, who brought the horse in and *deliberately*, mark that, hitched it outside Prinz's office? Who, why, for what purpose, to what end? Sayin' somethin'; provin' somethin', or just, as Prinz would have it, bein' decent? The good Samaritan, or...' She raised a hand with the index finger stiff and pointed, and added, 'a ghost from somebody's past?'

A beading of soft sweat glistened on Doc's brow. 'What you sayin' there, Shamrock? You suggestin' as how–'

'I'm puttin' two things to you, Doc.' Shamrock came to her feet, crossed to the window, and stared into the dusty, shadow-hugged sprawl of the street. 'What's the chances of what happened to Dusty Bing's horse bein' the work of a do-goodin' fella with a deep, lovin' feelin' for horses he happens to cross on his travels, and who just *happens* to be there when Dusty's mount shows up? You givin' me odds?'

Doc shook his head.

''Course you ain't. And you're givin' me even less than nothin' figurin' that this mysterious Samaritan then delivers the horse to Prinz, hitches it at his office and simply rides away into the night. Good work done ... horse safe and in care ... no reward asked, none expected. Time to go lookin' for the next unfortunate victim!' Shamrock turned, slapped her backside, and smiled cynically. 'Huh, my butt for a bag of bad beans!'

Doc swallowed. 'So?' he murmured.

'So, I don't believe none of it. Not a lousy word. There ain't a drifter nowhere, nohow, would do that without lookin' for a purse, free booze and one of the gals for the night. Not one, from here to ... God alone knows where. It ain't human nature as it is out here.' Shamrock's stare deepened into Doc's sweating face. 'Such a fella don't exist – but a ghost might.'

A flat, awkward silence fell between them. Shamrock adjusted the fit of her tight dress, and winced. 'Need to lose some weight,' she muttered absently. She gazed at Doc. 'Hey, cheer up there, old friend,' she smiled. 'We ain't all through yet. We've still got my deal with Denes in our favour. If I can pull that off–'

'And that's another problem,' said Doc carefully, raising his tired eyes to Shamrock's face. 'George Wickham's got a plan...'

He told her in some detail of the storekeeper's proposed scheme to get a man aboard the supplies wagon and out of town in search of help.

'Rubbish!' flared Shamrock, stepping from the window to the door. She brushed a stray hair from her shoulders, turned and stared hard at Doc.

'You're goin' to have to scupper that before it even gets started. Don't know how you're goin' to do it – and I don't much care – but you've gotta do it, Doc. Hell, the wagon's due in another day. We need them guns, and that means I need Denes to myself. Anythin' messes that up and Prinz will let the lead loose like he was havin' a hoedown in a funeral parlour!' She sat on the bed again, facing Doc, and took his hands in hers. 'Stop Wickham, Doc, at any price...'

That night drifted through an uneasy silence. Mission Rock slept, but fitfully. If anything the town only dozed.

Ma McCundrie closed the saloon bar later than usual. She had ordered the girls to their rooms long back. 'Fellas ain't in the mood,' she complained to Shamrock. 'Can't say I blame 'em. If I was a fella holed up here, I'd feel the same.' She had creaked the wicker wheelchair to the batwings, eased one aside and stared into the boot-black night. 'Ah, well,' she mused, 'human nature will out sooner or later, I suppose.'

'You for sharin' the last of this bottle with me, Ma?' offered Tinker Johnny from his usual table. 'Mite too much for me.'

'Why not,' said Ma, creaking the wheel-chair round. 'Why not, damn it! Got to seek our solace some place, ain't we, Tinker?'

'What's solace mean, Ma?' Tinker frowned, pouring two measures. 'I ain't never heard of solace before...'

Across the street in the scrubbed, scented cleanliness of his barber's shop, Picky Layton was watching the last of the bedroom lights flicker and go out as the girls snuggled down at last between sheets and found sleep. He sighed. Once again he had missed out; just simply not found the courage to speak to that pretty little brunette who always wore blue. One of these days, he hoped, she was going to be his. Not in the way the other fellows treated the girls. No, he would ask the girl if she would maybe have a drink with him, a meal even; maybe she would take a stroll with him one afternoon. No hidden intentions, she must understand. He was being gentlemanly, like a fellow should if he had any respect for a lady. Hell, he would bet the pretty little brunette had never been called a lady...

But meantime there were other matters to be considered. Very carefully and deeply considered. Prinz being the main target. He had to be taken care of, and soon, before it was all too late. And he, Picky Layton – or Ebenezer Greystock Layton, to give him his full name – was going to do it.

Do it too in a way that was so ridiculously simple as to be almost laughable. He was going to cut Prinz's throat. What else? He was a barber, darn it! Handling a cut-throat razor was his profession. Always had been. He was an expert. Damn it, he could cut any fellow's throat any time of asking once he had him in the chair.

So none of that fool talk about smuggling somebody aboard the supplies wagon, or getting hold of a gun and shooting it out as the youth had urged. No, Picky would do it the surprise way when Prinz came in for a shave – for which he never paid a cent, he reminded himself – and he had him at his mercy. That would be the moment. The few seconds of bewildering, inescapable shock and horror. The look on Prinz's face when the blood began to flow and he realized, all too late, that it was over. All over.

Picky smiled and took one last look at the darkened bedroom windows at the saloon. The pretty brunette shared the room second left. He knew that; he had seen her once, fleetingly, right there in that shiny blue dress.

'Ah, well,' he sighed, 'one day, one day...' And he closed the drapes sadly.

At the far end of the main street the lantern-light in Sheriff Prinz's office was never doused. He preferred it that way. And it was a whole sight safer than leaving things to chance. You never knew who might be the next fool to try something stupid. Particularly now, after what had happened earlier tonight.

That horse, that damned horse, hitched right outside his office there for everybody to see; fully saddled, tacked up, fresh as it might have come straight from the corral. And not a sign, sight, sound, not even a shadow of whoever might have trailed it in.

So who had? Not one of the town men, he would wager. A drifter? A drifter would have bargained a payment. A so-called Samaritan? Not out here. Not in a territory where a flick of eyes in the wrong direction at the wrong time could bring a whole stream of lead your way. No, this had been somebody else; somebody who had been intent on saying something, making a firm statement, delivering a message.

Prinz grunted, came wearily to his feet from the chair behind his desk, glanced briefly at his sleeping deputies sprawled like lizards round the office, and poured himself a drink. He gulped on it, sank the dregs and poured another.

Somebody who was living out there in the sand, he pondered on, strolling to the open door and stepping to the boardwalk? Somebody, certainly, who had the know-how to survive, and who was here for a reason, who had come with a purpose in mind and been lucky enough to fall across a ready-made calling-card. And somebody, thought Prinz, sipping at the drink, who knew him. A man from the past?

The sheriff grunted again, raised his eyes to the stars and the glass to his lips. 'Well, here's to you, fella, whoever you are, wherever you are. Lookin' forward to meetin' you. You bet!'

He smiled, then savoured the fire of the drink till it burned in his gut.

CHAPTER EIGHT

The arrival in town of the scheduled supplies wagon was an occasion not to be missed. Wickham's store would be replenished, sometimes with goods fresh out of the fashionable Eastern cities, sometimes with personal orders for folk who had waited close on a half-year, but mostly with those day-to-day, week-to-week necessities that kept and held a community together.

Watching from wherever they could gain a good vantage point to view the complete unloading and distribution were the ever curious folk, never ceasing to marvel how such luxuries ever came into being.

Top of most fellows' priorities was the restocking of McCundrie's saloon. Ma McCundrie would sit creaking in her wheelchair, noting meticulously the count of barrels, crates and boxes delivered, grunting only when she was satisfied the order had been met to her satisfaction, stored and locked safely away indoors. In spite of Sheriff Prinz and his gun-toting deputies.

Prinz had taken a surprisingly loose attitude to the arrival of the supplies wagon; he could see what was aboard, he could count it, watch it handled to its destination, but once that was through and Ma grunted her invitation to the wagon team to step up to the bar for some suitable refreshment, he lost interest. He would nod to the sulking sidekicks and step quickly back to his office. It was all a routine that went exactly to pattern. He had no need or cause to interfere.

For which on this particular morning, with the usual crowd gathered, Ma in place on the saloon boardwalk, the anxious hard drinkers already relishing the prospect of fresh brews, and George Wickham busy with his accounting, Doc was grateful. The storekeeper had made no attempt so far to approach Denes, and it needed to stay that way.

Only when Ma raised a hand to signal that the bar was open and he saw Denes making a beeline for Shamrock did he wipe a beading of sweat from his brow.

It looked as if Shamrock had got away

with it once again.

Ma had been quick to beckon Doc to her side once the crowd had dispersed and the street slipped back to its familiar heat-soaked emptiness.

'She's told me,' she said quietly as Doc helped her manoeuvre the chair into shade. 'You know what Shamrock's been doin' – is still doin',' she added, raising her eyes to the room above her. 'Got to admire her guts.'

'But at a price,' said Doc, beginning to sweat again. 'She shouldn't be doin' whatever it is she's doin'. No girl should.'

'And wouldn't be if I had my way. But we're playin' high stakes here, Doc. Guns are worth more than gold in this town. Don't have to tell you that.'

Doc pondered a moment. 'George Wickham's nursin' some crazy plan to bribe Denes into smugglin' somebody aboard the wagon on its return to Norricott.' He wiped his face with his bandanna. 'Can't let him get away with that.'

'Stop him,' said Ma, with a defiant creak of the chair. 'Any way you like. Tell him about the guns if you have to.' Her grey twinkling eyes scanned the street. 'What do you reckon on Dusty's horse showin' up again? Somethin' a mite odd there.'

'Very, and I ain't figured it yet. On the face of it, it don't make too much sense. But if it was somebody bein' just plain decent...' Doc shrugged. 'Least he could have stayed for a drink.'

Ma creaked the chair round to the 'wings. 'Keep your eyes open; find out what you can. Who knows, the fella might be back. Meanwhile, time to keep a watch on things in there – and rescue Shamrock soon as I can.' She gazed at Doc intently. 'Meet me again tonight. Here. We'll discuss what we're goin' to do with them guns.'

Doc nodded and went back to the fierce sunlight.

The long afternoon of that day idled through the heat-filled hours like a sore hound with no place to bed down.

Doc had paced the living-room of his neat clapboard home on the edge of town until he could stand the monotony of the movement no longer. He had taken to the rocker on his shadowed back porch, only to suffer the same restlessness, the same impatience with the heat, the silence broken from time to time by irate flies, the same air of close tension. Or was it fear? Had Mission Rock finally been driven by Prinz and his threats to a place where even the shadows might terrorize?

But how to break it, damn it, that was the problem. Wickham's crazy plan to smuggle a man out of town; Shamrock's terrible self-sacrifice for guns. Were these a way, or was there something else, something they had all overlooked? Or perhaps not yet met?

Doc might have driven himself to a still deeper lathering of sweat and confusion, or been tempted to sample his best whiskey, had there not been, eventually, a rap at the door to rouse him.

His visitor was the blacksmith, Hank Stone, a man in some state of agitation judging by his flushed, anxious appearance as he stood, shifting his weight from one leg to the other in the doorway.

'Hank,' Doc grinned, opening the door fully. 'Heck, you look a mite troubled there. Step inside. What in tarnation has happened?'

'That's the problem, Doc, I ain't rightly sure,' flustered Hank, removing his hat, only to twirl it through his hands like a hot coal. 'I just can't figure it.'

Doc eased the man to an easy-chair. 'Relax, Hank. God, you're sweatin' fit to melt.'

'You bet,' said the blacksmith, laying aside his hat to rummage for a bandanna. He mopped his face feverishly. 'Had a bit of a shock back there at my place.' He mopped again. Doc waited. 'Kinda took me by surprise – though it wouldn't for some. Nossir. Others wouldn't have reckoned. No need to. Why should they? Hell, I know to these things...' His voice drifted. His eyes glazed. 'You gotta believe that, Doc.'

Doc patted Hank's arm. 'Easy, easy. Take your time. Relax there.' He studied the man anxiously. 'What say we have a drink, eh? I got some real good whiskey here. A special. Ma found it for me. Know what, it came on her personal recommendation. And that's sayin' somethin'!'

Hank managed a weak half-smile, relaxed in the chair and took the measure from Doc with murmured thanks.

'That's better,' soothed Doc. He waited again, watching the man carefully. He judged his moment:

'Now, let's be hearin', fella, just what's lathered you up like this. You ready to tell me?'

Hank closed his eyes for a moment, and smiled. 'Better,' he said. 'Much better.' He sipped at the measure.

'Then tell me,' said Doc earnestly. 'Get it off your chest.'

Hank sat forward, cupping the drink in his hands. 'That horse,' he began, 'the one hitched outside Prinz's office. I took it in, like you know, settled it for the night, reckonin' for it needin' calm and feed and a decent rest before I got to takin' a closer look come sun-up.' He rolled the glass between the palms of his hands and stared into the swirl of liquid. 'Damn it, I knew that horse since Dusty first brought it in. One of my family, you might say. I know 'em all, Doc. That's my life, my livin'.'

'And nobody better, Hank,' said Doc. 'We all appreciate that, the whole town.'

Hank finished the drink in one gulp. 'Anyhow, I got to the mount first thing. Time for it to have a real rub and brush down, nice and easy. And it was then that I smelled it. No mistakin'. Knew it straight off.'

'Knew what? Smelled what?' frowned Doc.

Hank came to his feet and placed his glass on the table. 'The liniment. That horse had been tended out there in the sands by somebody who had the liniment. It's special. Real special. Only ever crossed it once and that was years back. My pa told me of it.'

63

Doc's frown deepened. 'Sorry, Hank, I ain't fully with you. Explain.'

'When a horse gets tired, all-in tired after hard-ridin' and sweatin' up, it aches, every darn muscle. You know to that, Doc. Times when there ain't a limb of you that's your own. Know what I mean?'

'You bet I do. Get 'em through here every day.'

'And the Indians up North knew too. Still do. They knew to the days when bad snows and hard goin' took a horse to the limits.' Hank smiled softly. 'But they sure as hell knew how to ease the strain and have that horse fresh as popped seed the next day. It was the liniment that did it. Made up to their own special recipe. And only them Indians up North knew to it – save those so favoured they cared to share it with. Well, I'm tellin' you, Doc, that horse of Dusty's had been so treated by a fella who had the liniment right there with him. Knew how to apply it. Had done it times before. And, my hand on the Good Book, so help me, definitely ain't from these parts. Not nohow.'

Hank stiffened. 'Mission Rock's got one helluva stranger takin' a very close interest in us, you mark my word to that. I wonder why?'

CHAPTER NINE

Doc was already late for his meeting with Ma at the saloon when he had at last closed and locked the front door to his home and hurried through the gathering night gloom to the brighter glow of the main street.

Hank's account of what he had discovered on Dusty Bing's horse had only served to add to the clutter of confusions swimming through his head. Shamrock's plan to obtain guns ... George Wickham's scheming to smuggle somebody out of town ... and now this. And just what might be turning through Ma's head right now?

It had taken Doc the better part of the afternoon and into early evening to settle Hank's own confusion – and sometimes wild speculations – and eventually to calm him into the promise that he would go take another look at the horse, keep a close watch on it, and maybe get to examining the saddle in some closer detail.

'No sayin' to what that might reveal,' Doc had said, doing his level best not to get too fancifully speculative himself. Heck, it might prove yet to be all a perfectly decent gesture of goodwill by somebody who was just passing through – and wanted to keep it that way. 'A tall shot to call,' Doc had concluded without a deal of conviction in his voice, 'but such things do happen. Oh, yes, they surely do.'

Except, of course, that Doc did not believe it, and neither, he suspected, did Hank. Nevertheless, the blacksmith had left. 'We'll see, eh, Doc, we'll see. But I'll be back. You bet. There's somethin' ... oh, yes, there's somethin'.'

And privately, Doc did not doubt it.

Meanwhile, there was Ma, waiting right there in her back room, a fresh bottle of whiskey opened and ready to be poured, her eyes as piercing as ever, her mind razor-sharp, and that creaking wicker wheelchair never still, not for a moment.

Ma was unusually deep, and preoccupied as Doc closed the door to her private room and took his place at the table facing her. He watched as she poured two measures to the waiting glasses. The room was warm, almost balmy with a faint hint of past cigar-smoke, the drift of Ma's lavender scent and the heady tang of the freshly opened bottle of best whiskey. The heavy furniture, drapes, ornaments and favoured bric-a-brac seemed to press closer through the dim lantern-glow, as if anxious to touch.

'You look troubled,' said Ma, without looking at Doc. She finished pouring, placed the bottle aside and gestured for Doc to take his drink. 'Somethin' new botherin' you?' she added, creaking back into the wicker wheelchair as she sampled her drink.

'Maybe.' Doc shrugged, swirling the measure in the glass. 'I can't be sure. Can't see yet how I could ever be sure, not right now.'

Ma's chair creaked. 'Care to get it off your chest?' she asked, sipping quietly. 'We've got the time.'

'Maybe, I will,' said Doc. 'Yeah, maybe so, seein' as how it might just come to count in the way of things.' He sampled the drink liberally. 'It's like this. Hank Stone came to see me this afternoon...'

Ma listened intently and carefully to Doc through the twenty minutes it took him to relate Hank's account of his discovery at the livery. 'He's gone back now to take a real good look at the saddle. Maybe he'll find somethin' there.'

Ma waited until Doc had finished his

drink. She delved into a side pocket of her full-length, high-necked black dress, drew a cheroot from a tooled leather case, lit it and blew a thin line of smoke into the soft haze of the lantern's glow. 'And what do you reckon?' she murmured, her eyes brightening like sudden lights.

'Hard to say.' Doc sighed, rolling his empty glass between his hands. 'Can't argue with Hank's figurin' of the liniment. Hell, he should know. But that in itself don't prove a thing. All it tells us is that whoever trailed Dusty's mount back to town probably came from the north, or had at least been there sometime back. And that, frankly, ain't nothin' unusual. And yet... And yet, I just get this feelin'...' He placed the glass on the table, slapped his knees and leaned back. 'There just ain't no tellin'. Let's wait. Meantime, what of Shamrock and her plan?'

Ma blew another line of smoke, this time deliberately as if hoping it would speak. Her eyes gleamed behind the haze. 'Shamrock ain't in no fit state to see anybody right now,' she said in little more than a slow murmur.

Doc leaned forward. 'She needs me. I can tell she does.' He came to his feet. 'I'll go get my bag—'

'You'll sit down!' snapped Ma, the chair

creaking like wheezing breath. 'You'll pour yourself another drink, and you'll listen.'

Doc grunted and sat down. 'But if she's–'

'She needs to sleep right now. Best thing for her – then you can see her. Meantime...' Ma leaned across the table to pour two fresh measures. 'Meantime, the job's done. We have the guns. All we need. They're hidden and nobody save you and me, Mopps and Shamrock know a thing about em.'

'What about Denes?' asked Doc, anxiously.

'Denes has had his fill, and more, though he don't yet know it. You can leave him to me.' Ma sampled a generous half of her drink, savoured it, closed her eyes for a moment, and smiled. 'We're gettin' close, real close. But what I want you to hear is the plan from here on. So relax, enjoy the drink and listen up...'

'Give me a head-count,' said Sheriff Prinz, stepping to the deepest shadows on the boardwalk fronting the mercantile. 'Who's where?'

Chine Billet eased to the sheriff's side, cradled his Winchester and spat into the street dirt. 'Our boys are close. Mouthy's back of the buildings across there, workin' his way to the livery. He'll keep an eye on the blacksmith most of the night.' He spat again, accepted a cheroot from Prinz and waited for him to light it. 'Skeets is where you'd expect Skeets to be – with the girls. My bettin' right now would be he's got two of Ma's prettiest, one on each knee. That's where they'll stay 'til Skeets fancies otherwise.'

Prinz grunted, drew on his cheroot and blew an angry curl of smoke to the starlit night. He wiped the sweat from his brow. 'Women will be his downfall,' he murmured, hissing out the words like an annoyed rattler. 'One of these days...' He blew more smoke. 'What about Doc? Where's he?'

'Holed up with Ma in her backroom. He was home all afternoon. Had a visit from Stone, but I don't rate it none.' Billet shifted from the deeper darkness to the edge of the boardwalk and stared into the night. 'Otherwise, all is quiet. Only one I ain't seen since that supplies wagon hit town is Shamrock.'

'She'll have been with Denes,' said Prinz. 'He took a shine to her. She'll surface later.'

'Guess so.' Billet shifted his stare to a controlled gaze up and down the street. 'Town gets to sleepin' early these nights. Ain't more than a handful in the saloon. Ma'll be complainin'! Mebbe she'll double the price to Skeets. Serve him right!' He watched the drift of his cheroot-smoke, then narrowed his eyes. 'I speak too soon. The undertaker ain't restin' up at home. He's headin' this way right now – and he's seen us.'

Prinz stepped from the shadows as Elmer Puce, still struggling into the formality of his dark jacket, approached at a brisk pace.

'That you there, Sheriff?' called the undertaker. 'Just the man. Time for you to get to some real investigatin' hereabouts.'

'What's the problem, Elmer?' asked Prinz, stepping to the street to lean on a hitching-rail. 'You look a mite mithered there.'

'You bet,' said Puce, coming to a sweating halt a few yards from the sheriff. He stared hard at him for a moment, then glanced quickly at Billet. 'How come,' he began, the sweat beading heavily on his cheeks, 'how come somebody gets to stealin' a coffin from my back yard?'

'Am I hearin' you right there?' croaked Prinz, easing clear of the rail to stand fully upright.

'You bet you are, mister,' snapped Puce. 'I'll say it again: somebody has stolen a coffin from my back yard. Stolen it tonight.

71

Not an hour ago. Did a count myself in readiness. And there's one missin'. It's gone. Vanished. Somebody's taken it. And best quality pine at that. So who was it? More to the point, what you goin' to do about it?'

CHAPTER TEN

Though the hour was already late and darkness had long since closed in like a cloak, Mission Rock was not much for sleeping that night.

News of the raid on Elmer Puce's yard and the disappearance of a coffin – unused at that – had spread quickly, filling the saloon bar at McCundrie's with a crowd of the anxious, the curious, the downright scared and those who readily joined in the suddenly excited drinking. Elmer, of course, was at the centre of the debate that flowed back and forth across the bar.

'I'm tellin' you straight up – every last man of you – what's goin' on in this town just ain't natural. Nossir. Not one measly bit.'

'Tell that to Sheriff Prinz and them dogs of his,' said a man with a wheezing cough and a running nose. He fumbled for a bandanna and plastered it to his face in a fit of sneezes and splutters.

'Lucky for you they ain't here now,' chimed a man at the bar.

'Holed up in Prinz's office wonderin' what the hell to do,' added another, finishing his drink and ordering up his fourth.

Mopps, the barman, obliged, then turned his attention to the next customer.

'But who in the name of blisterin' rock would want an empty coffin?' asked a lean man, pushing his hat to the back of his head to scratch his baldness.

A man with no teeth and a permanent dribble at the corner of his mouth, spluttered, 'Somebody with a body to get rid of.'

'Or expectin' one,' murmured Ma Mc-Cundrie, creaking her wheelchair from the shadows.

The bar fell silent. Smoke hung like sad, funeral breath. Mopps stopped serving. A bar-girl removed a young man's pawing hand from her thigh. A dog, dozing on the boards at the batwings, nose to the fresher air outside, sloped off. The man without teeth dribbled. Ma creaked her wheelchair to the full light of the lanterns and gazed over the faces in the gathering.

'Well, you want me to spell it out?' she growled.

'Ain't too certain as to what you're sayin' there, Ma,' said the man at the bar.

The man with the cough wheezed, 'Me neither,' and buried his face in the bandanna.

Picky Layton eased forward. 'Heck, let's not get to supposin' things we ain't no right to be supposin'.'

'And just what dumbhead jumble of nothin' is that supposed to mean, Mr Layton?' snapped Ma, creaking to the bar and gesturing to Mopps to pour her a measure from the bottle no one ever saw.

'Well, I–' blustered Picky.

'Well, I nothin', mister. It's all gettin' obvious to me that–'

'Hold it right there, Ma,' said Doc Cherry, appearing from a darker corner of the bar, George Wickham and Hank Stone a step behind him. 'I'm reckonin' on what you have in mind, Ma – that the appearance of Dusty's horse hitched at the sheriff's rail, and the disappearance–'

'Stealin',' interrupted Elmer.

'Stealin',' continued Doc, 'of the coffin from Mr Puce's yard might – just might mark you – have been the work of one and the same person.'

The saloon bar gathering came to life. An old man aimed a careful line of spittle to a spittoon, heard it sink and said, 'Got to say I'd go along with that.'

The men fidgeted, murmured and muttered among themselves. Some refilled empty glasses. Some called to Mopps for a fresh bottle. One man broke open a new deck of cards and began to shuffle them aimlessly, dropping four to the floor. The young man's hand advanced delicately to the bar-girl's thigh, and stayed. She seemed unaware.

Doc looked directly at Ma, and winked. She winked back. No mention of buried guns, no reaction from the storekeeper and his plan to smuggle somebody out of town aboard the supplies wagon. The town men were suddenly, intently focused and concentrated. Sonofabitch, there might be a fellow out there who might, could, perhaps would.

'Hey, we're walkin' on clouds here,' called the young man standing now behind the bar-girl, his hands clamped to both her thighs. 'Picky's right, Doc, that's all fond supposin', chicken-cacklin' storytellin'. Are you, or anybody else here, seriously suggestin' that there could be somebody out there who knows this town, knows Prinz and is personally – one man alone – wagin' some kinda vendetta for reasons we could never begin to know let alone fathom?' He took a deep breath. Sweat blossomed and sparkled on his brow. The hands on the girl's thighs dampened. 'Gotta say it, Doc, but all that's just apple-pie in a goddamn stream of dreamin' sky.'

The man with the cards dealt himself a duff hand.

Mopps cleaned down the bar without looking where the cloth was going.

George Wickham hooked his thumbs into his waistcoat, glared quickly at Doc, then at Ma, and wondered whether he was going crazy. Picky Layton's face broke into a lathering of sweat.

Doc sighed. 'Well, I ain't sayin' nothin' for certain. All I'm tryin' to do is–'

'Drinks on the house!' shouted Ma, creaking her chair across the room. 'And there ain't no charge tonight for fondlin' the girls.' She glanced round her. *'Fondlin'* I said, *and fondlin'* I mean!'

The gathering relaxed and headed four-deep to the bar. Doc moved to the batwings and passed through to the boardwalk. He stiffened, breathed deep on the smoke-free air and felt his shirt grow sticky across his back. 'Damn the heat,' he muttered, reaching for his bandanna and mopping his neck.

Only then did he notice the dark, silhouetted shape of the figure moving through the shadows towards the sheriff's office.

'Don't pander to me none, Doc. Just do it. Tell me.' Shamrock leaned back on the pillows piled high behind her, adjusted the nightdress across her breasts, and stared hard at Doc Cherry. 'Well?' she glared.

'No good'll come of me tellin' you to rest,' said Doc.

'Too damned right! Go on.'

'There's an awful lot of bruisin' there, Shamrock, and there's ... well, other things.' Doc paused. 'Damn it, woman, you need carin' for.'

'You offerin'?' Shamrock smiled.

Doc straightened and took a slow, thoughtful turn around the room. He halted. 'Yes,' he said quietly. 'Yes, I am – if you'll do exactly as I say when I say it. Which, of course, you won't!'

'Very likely.' Shamrock smiled again. 'But there ain't the time, is there?' Her face relaxed, hardened, turned greyer, the lips thinner as if planed away. 'Tell me, what's happenin', and quick. Then I'll do as you say.'

'I ain't never argued with you, my dear, and I sure as hell ain't for startin' now. So... Well, here's how it is: Ma's got a plan for the use of the guns. I'll tell you later. Meanwhile, a coffin's gone missin', probably stolen, from Elmer's yard, and ... there's somethin' I ain't yet mentioned to anyone.'

Shamrock leaned forward, the nightdress falling helplessly from her breasts. 'Now that does interest me. Tell me....'

There was an air of smoky gloom in Sheriff Prinz's dimly lit office. Two of the three deputies, Skeets Murphy and Mouthy Kline, lounged in a half-dozing, half-awake stupor. Mouthy snored, stirred, grunted, snored again until Murphy's boot cracked across his shin and roused him in a state of sweat and spinning images. Only Chine Billet watched the night, the empty street and the faint, flickering lights at McCundrie's saloon. Prinz simply brooded, lost in dark thoughts, and stared into a fast diminishing bottle of whiskey.

'Quiet enough now,' said Chine, aiming a line of spittle into the dirt, before turning and sauntering back into the office. He

78

stared for a moment at the snoring deputies. 'Ain't they a sight for sore eyes,' he quipped, pouring himself a drink from the bottle in front of Murphy. 'Don't they give you a sense of security, eh? My, my, we could have another half-dozen coffins whipped from under our eyes and they, bless their varnished innards, wouldn't know a damn thing.' He sank the drink and poured himself another. 'They need a roustin', boss,' he said, facing Prinz. 'You figure they need a roustin'?'

Prinz grunted, wiped his eyes with the backs of his hands, and came wearily to his feet. 'And mebbe they'll get just that if we don't get to nailin' the sonofabitch who's roundin' up horses and stealin' coffins.'

'You reckonin' for it bein' the same fella?' Billet frowned. 'Stretchin' it some, ain't it? Hell, might just be a kinda coincidence – you know, a decent type returns a stray, wanderin' horse, and some skit-headed young 'uns hereabouts get to givin' old Puce a scare, tweakin' him up the backside. Kids do that, don't they? Mischief. I'd figure for that.' He replaced the bottle, flicked Murphy's hat over his face and kicked the chair supporting Kline's legs from under him. 'Shift your lazy butts there! Darn me, place could be burnin' down!'

Kline stirred and groaned. 'I ain't smellin' nothin' burnin',' he groaned. Billet grinned and slapped the man's back. 'That's on account of this place bein' full of your own stink, Mouthy! You don't never smell nothin' but yourself. Time you launched out on a full tub-bath. Some decent soap thrown in along of it, always assumin' that barberin' fella's carryin' enough stock. I'd reckon for it takin'–'

'Cut the personal stuff, mister,' growled Kline. 'T'ain't called for. I'll get to takin' a bath when I figure it's time to–'

The four men stiffened and were suddenly silent, unmoving, at the sound of a thud somewhere at the back of the office.

Prinz's eyes narrowed. He licked slowly at salty sweat. Billet gripped his Winchester. Kline stood up and hitched his pants, his eyes tight on the shadows. Skeets Murphy's hand dropped instinctively to the butt of his holstered Colt.

'What was that?' rasped Prinz, still licking at the beading sweat. 'Mouthy, go take a look.'

The deputy grunted, settled his hat, drew a gun in his right hand, and slid like a shadow to the deeper night beyond the smoky office.

CHAPTER ELEVEN

It was close on two-o'clock in the morning, with the moon still high and steady, the stars like watchful eyes from an ink-black sky, when George Wickham tapped anxiously and persistently at Doc Cherry's back-room window.

It was all of ten past when Doc came to, gathered himself and slipped from under the single sheet covering his naked body.

'Who in tarnation's out there?' he croaked, grabbing a hand-towel as a fumbled loin-cloth as he staggered to the window.

He peered, rubbed at the sand-streaked pane and eventually, with a groaning sigh, recognized the sweating face of the store-keeper.

'You'd better have one helluva good reason for rousin' me at this hour, George,' he said, once Wickham was indoors and Doc had struggled into a pair of crumpled black trousers. 'I ain't for bein' woken by somebody tappin' at back-room windows. Damn it, man, there's a perfectly good knocker on

81

the front door – and in thirty years of doctorin' to the good folk of Mission Rock I ain't failed yet, not once, to hear it.'

Doc paused, breathless, beginning to sweat and still with his trousers threatening to drop to his ankles. 'So what's the problem?' he asked, running his tongue over dry lips, his gaze tight on Wickham's face.

'Sorry about the window,' began the storekeeper, twisting his hat through his fingers. 'But it's Prinz. Well, it ain't Prinz so much as one of his deputies ... that scumbag Mouthy Kline... It's him.'

'What do you mean, it's him?' frowned Doc. 'What's he done, f'cris'sake?'

George Wickham swallowed. 'Gotten himself killed. Throat cut, clean as slicin' through bacon. And he's right here in town, middle of the street, in the coffin that went missin' out of Elmer's yard...'

Doc Cherry's shirt-tails were still flapping from the top of his trousers when he reached the already crowded main street.

He lowered his medicine-bag to the ground and squinted into the swinging patterns of light and shadow from newly primed and lit lanterns. 'Don't nobody ever get to sleepin' in this town?' he murmured as the storekeeper sweated to his side and pushed his hat to the back of his head.

'Hell, would you just look at that,' said Wickham, gulping so that his knotted tie-lace at his collar wobbled on the bounce of his Adam's apple. 'Would you just believe it...'

'Not if I weren't seein' it for myself,' croaked Doc.

'Me neither,' echoed Wickham glancing quickly to left and right as the town crowd swelled, women and night-clad young ones snuggling at their parents' sides.

A dog loped over to the street dirt, scenting the smell of a dead body, nosed, whined pitifully for a moment as if in solemn sympathy, and cringed away. Men stared, some scratching, some mopping at cold sweat; others watching furtively for someone to move. A tall, moon-eyed youth muttered something about 'evil spirits' but was hushed and shouldered out of sight. An elderly woman, wrapped in a deep shawl, sniffed at a bottle of smelling-salts and fumbled in her night-clothes for a fan.

Sheriff Prinz stood alone at the foot of the coffin where the body of his deputy, Mouthy Kline, fully clothed, eyes wide, mouth gaping, blood congealing like an oozing slime at his slashed throat, was stiffening fast. Death seeped and thickened on the balmy night air.

'Somebody'll pay,' hissed Prinz to himself, but conscious of Chine Billet and Skeets Murphy shifting only a step behind him. The sheriffs voice rose as he lifted his head and, sweat pouring from his scarred and pock-marked face, yelled, 'In fact, you'll all pay, every last one of you!' He glared round him. 'This street is goin' to run with blood. Your blood, damn you! Damn you all ... into hell ... into bloody, damnation's writhin' hell!'

It was a full ten minutes before Prinz had yelled and shouted himself out of breath and just stood, silent, sweating, mouthing, twitching, at the foot of Elmer's planed and sanded pine coffin.

No one, it seemed, had moved. A woman had sniffed back tears, but not for Mouthy; more perhaps for her family's fate. A girl, still in her nightdress, had shuddered as if cold and fallen willingly enough into the hug of a man behind her. The elderly woman had replaced the smelling-salts, huffed disapprovingly at the whole sorry scene, and hustled herself homewards. 'You bet your last sweet dollar the Lord above is watchin'... Oh, yes, you bet to it. And Hallelujah to that! Glory, glory, Hallelujah, glory, glory...' She had chorused until out of sight.

Hank Stone, Picky Layton and Tinker Johnny, had lost no time during Prinz's rantings to gather close to Doc and the storekeeper.

'I got this deep-gutted, squirmy feelin' that we ain't alone,' Picky had begun to the nodding agreement of the others. 'It's a feelin' that's spreadin' fast.'

'I'll vouch to that,' added Tinker, scratching furiously at four days' sweat-matted stubble. 'Ain't a livin' soul in this town would do a thing like we're witnessin' to right here in the street in front of our own eyes. Nossir. Not a soul. And you can't name me one. Ask anybody. Just anybody.'

'Easy, fellas, easy,' urged the storekeeper, placing a quietening finger to his lips. 'If we get to talkin' too loud—'

'Goddamnit, George, we ain't babes!' Hank Stone frowned, ripping his shirt from his chest with a sigh of relief as the sweat coursed down his body. 'I figure we can all see, everybody, every man, boy and woman crowdin' this street, that there's a bein' some place – Lord above knows where or how –

who's takin' one almighty keen interest in Mission Rock and Sheriff Prinz. And who, in fact, is responsible for the return of Dusty's horse, that body stinkin' fit to sicken you right there, and who ain't done yet. Oh, no, who's only just gettin' started...'

On that night it was to be another hour before the street had emptied, Elmer Puce ordered the coffin and its grisly contents to be carried to his yard. Prinz and his deputies waited, watching every movement, from the boardwalk fronting the sheriffs office.

Prinz had gestured for Doc to join him. 'Ain't no need for an examination there, eh, Doc?' he had said, lighting a cheroot. 'Plain enough.' He had blown smoke and glared from behind it. 'Killed outright, wouldn't you say? Deliberate. Planned. And not by some first-timer, eh, Doc? Oh, no. This fella sure as little green apples knew what he was about. Yessir. He knew, every goddamn inch of the way.' He blew more smoke. 'Kinda clinical, weren't it? Would that be your professional opinion, Doc?'

Doc Cherry had swallowed, once again easing his bag to the street dirt as he stared at Prinz above him on the boardwalk. 'You askin' me if the fella who killed Mouthy

Kline is a professional killer? Is that what you're askin'? Then the answer's yes, I'd reckon so. This ain't the first time he's slit a fella's throat, and not raised so much as a whimper in the doin' of it. He's done it before, and like as not he'll do it again.'

Prinz had examined the glowing tip of his cheroot, flicked a drifting of ash to the still night air, watched it fall like moondust, and smiled. 'You figure for him bein' a town man?' he asked slowly, his eyes settling tight on Doc's face.

Doc took his time adjusting the last of shirt-tails into his trousers. 'Mebbe not. In fact, as like as not. But I sure as hell figure for him knowin' you, Mr Prinz. That I am certain of ... professionally speakin', you understand.'

CHAPTER TWELVE

Doc Cherry mumbled and muttered to himself as he emptied the contents of his medicine-bag, checked each item against what he knew he had in stock in the cabinet facing him, grunted, then, slamming an empty bottle on the table, sighed, stood back and lit the last of his best cigars.

He relished the easy aroma of the smoke, the gentle satisfaction of its taste. Quality, he mused, the tobacco-leaf had quality. Something sadly missing from Mission Rock at this particular time. Damnit, the whole place was beginning to smell. He cut himself short, grunted again and concentrated on the cigar.

Time to rest, to think, to plan, he thought, stepping away from the table and the scattered contents of his bag. 'Later,' he murmured, 'later....'

His mind drifted; images crowded, broke away. His eyes closed, opened wide, closed again, flickered. He ran a hand over his face. No time for sleeping. He drew quickly on the cigar, poured a measure of whiskey, and eased his way slowly, thoughtfully round the silent, shadow-spilled living-room.

Nothing else for it, he resolved, not for the first time since leaving Sheriff Prinz at his office, it had to be done. And now, tonight, or what remained of it.

He would pack a bag of essential supplies, saddle up his mount and ride out to the sands. If there was somebody out there – and he was near certain as he could be that there was – he would find him. He would find out who he was, why he was here, what he intended and just why, damn it, he was intent on doing it. Could the fellow know of what was happening in the town, of Prinz's iron grip on it, the murder of innocent folk? If he did, then surely...

Doc finished his drink, drew still deeper on the cigar, watched the smoke climb, curl and shred like old lace, and narrowed his gaze on the shadowed room. No more thinking. Just get to the doing; get back to the bag, what was needed... Think man, think.

The living-room clock clunked and chimed the hour. The still heavy air thickened. The last of the night began to weaken. Silence brooded.

The sun was climbing, the haze low and clinging like a soft mist as Ma McCundrie creaked her wheelchair through the bat-wings to the heavily shaded boardwalk.

She enjoyed this time of the day. It was cooler, quieter; the street was invariably empty, even the dogs had loped away to sleep. No one stirred, unless they had good need to. It would be another hour before Mopps began his slow cleaning and sweeping, stocking and checking of the saloon in preparation for another day's trade. The bar girls would be relishing their time alone between clean sheets. Shamrock, she hoped, would be feeling a deal easier.

This was her time – a time to reflect, smoke a gentle cheroot, sip quietly at her medicinal measure of best French brandy, and wonder just how in hell Mission Rock was ever going to get back to being just an ordinary town for ordinary folk to live out their ordinary lives in decent, law-abiding times. And right now she had no answers, save those that did not involve death, shoot-outs, blood-baths and destruction, only to be left with a town that was a town no more.

Her one spark of hope, a glimmer of something that might become a whole sight more important, was the possibility, how-ever faint, that there just might be an unknown person somewhere about with an unexpected interest in Mission Rock.

The death of Mouthy Kline and the bizarre return of his body in the stolen coffin – 'simply borrowed' as Elmer Puce had later described it – had not been the doing of a town man, of that Ma was in no doubt. But she was equally certain that somebody, a stranger, was close and watching the town and the events taking place here with an unusual interest. And that, she reckoned, was putting it mildly. Could be...

But it was at that moment that Ma's early morning contemplations were broken at the sight of George Wickham skulking nervously through the low haze as he headed for the saloon.

'Figured you should know soonest,' the storekeeper gulped, still casting an anxious gaze over the street, 'I've just seen Doc Cherry ridin' out for the sands from back of his home.' He moved closer to Ma, carrying a chair behind him, settled it, sat down, leaned forward, and murmured, 'Wouldn't surprise me one bit if he ain't for takin' up my plan.' He tapped the side of his nose. 'Could be, eh? Could be.'

'What could be, George?' said Ma, without lifting her gaze from the street.

'My plan to get a man out of town, go get some help to see us out of this mess. It's the only way. I'd reckoned for smugglin' somebody out on the supplies wagon. Recruitin' that fella Denes to help us. But he don't seem concerned with nothin' save Shamrock. Which reminds me, she ain't been around. Rumour was spreadin' to say as how she–'

'Forget it,' said Ma brusquely, setting up a series of protesting creaks from the chair as she adjusted herself, finished the brandy, drew on the cheroot and blew a thin line of smoke into the morning haze. 'Stay clear of Shamrock for a day or so, and leave Doc to his own devices.' She eyed the storekeeper like an ageing hawk. 'There's things happenin'. Just stay low and keep out of Prinz's way.'

'But how–'

Ma swung the wheelchair round to the batwings. 'Do like I say – and wait.'

Hank Stone and Elmer Puce had sat for close on an hour, through a whole pot of fresh coffee, watching the sun come up over the sands. Neither of them had spoken; neither had moved from their seats on the straw-bales at the open stable doors where the light streamed in shafts through the thin morning haze. They were content enough for the moment to just sit, watch the emergence of the far horizon, and be alone with their thoughts.

It was Elmer who eventually broke the silence.

'Didn't sleep none after dealin' with that coffin and Kline's body,' he began, running a slow tongue over his lips. 'Didn't feel the need.' He paused. 'I ain't usually so taken. Must've been the occasion.'

The blacksmith gave him a quick sidelong glance. 'Wouldn't figure it so much an occasion. A blessin' more like. Kline's one less, and that counts in my book.'

Elmer was a long time answering while his grey, thoughtful eyes scanned the sprawl of the sands, and the fingers of one hand drummed quietly across his knee. 'I got to thinkin' in that time, that whoever knifed him knew his business. I seen shootin's and knifin's to fill a book, and this, take it from me, was good. Oh, yes, real good.' Elmer's tongue ran hurriedly across his lips, curled and disappeared. 'I reckon for Mouthy Kline never known' a damn thing, which is a shame when you come to think of it. Kline should have died knowin' it, feelin' it, so that he was–'

'Yeah, well, mebbe,' calmed Hank, putting his mug aside. 'I just take your word for it, Elmer, same as you take mine for what I've told you about that liniment used on Dusty's horse. Now that, I know, was a ridin' fella's knowledge. Somebody who knew how to keep a mount goin' way beyond the limits.'

'That's it then, ain't it?' said Elmer with a sudden stiffening of his shoulders. 'Put like that – poolin', you might say, the experience of our brains – we know there's somebody out there in them godforsaken sands who's comin' for Prinz ... twist by twist, rattle by rattle, like some hate-gorged sidewinder.' Elmer turned to gaze wide-eyed at Hank. 'Now just who do you figure has purpose enough and the guts to be that kinda fella? Just who?'

His tongue sank from his lips, his fingers lay flat and lifeless on his knees, and his grey, thoughtful eyes went back to watching the haze, the sands and the far horizon. All he said was, 'Hell.'

CHAPTER THIRTEEN

The sun was high, hot and fearless when Doc Cherry eventually reached the shade of the only outcrop of rock he had seen in ten miles of hard riding.

He eased the mare to a halt, patted her neck, murmured to her soft snort, and slid from the saddle. He was careful with his canteen of water; he sipped, then soaked a rag and soothed the horse's mouth. She snorted again, tossed her head and nuzzled his shoulder.

'I know, I know,' said Doc, fixing the canteen back on his saddle, then removing his hat to soak the sweat on his head with a clean bandanna. 'Feel the same, gal, but I gotta see this through somehow...'

His voice trailed away as he mopped the bandanna over his face and narrowed his gaze on the shimmering sand-locked land surrounding him. Damn all to be seen that meant a deal, he thought, lifting a hand to shade his eyes against the glare. Sand, rock, scattered stone; distances that seemed to fade into nowhere. Unseen horizons beyond horizons.

He grunted, swished the bandanna and soaked up more sweat.

Maybe he had misjudged this whole situation, he mused, settling his back against a shaded boulder. Hell, what real chance was there of finding somebody out here, who might be anywhere in hundreds of square miles of sand and rock, and who had been smart enough, silent enough, deft as an old ghost, to shiver down Sheriff Prinz's spine like dribbled ice-water? If he could do that, be in and out of Mission Rock without a soul setting eyes on him; if that was the fellow he was trying to track without a sniff of a hint to his whereabouts, then he was steer-spooked stupid.

And best admit it right now. Do the decent thing and save his horse more sweat and effort. Save himself from the misery of these goddamn sands. Just get back to town, keep a closer eye on Prinz, tend to Shamrock, look to those who needed him most.

He grunted again and moved to mount up. And then he halted, one foot in a stirrup, froze for a moment before easing back to stand fully upright. A shadow was creeping towards him. A long, lean shadow that was deep and dark and certain of its progress.

A shadow, Doc decided, you did not argue with.

Sheriff Prinz stood on the boardwalk fronting his office, his eyes glinting in the shade as he scanned the main street, from the forge and livery at one end, past Ma McCundrie's saloon to the timber-yard and sprawling corral at the other. The sun was already high in the cloudless sky, the heat clamoured, stray flies buzzed, a lone hawk cruised the silent blue above him, a town dog skulked to an alley and disappeared.

'Time will come,' he murmured, conscious of Skeets Murphy and Chine Billet flanking him, 'when this whole place will die, and there won't be nothin', not a stick of it, left to say what it was. There'll be only the dust of dead men. Just dust, blowin' on them coolin' winds come nightfall. The ghosts of Mission Rock lost in them god-forsaken sands.'

'You want me and Chine here should get started?' said Murphy, cradling a Winchester across him, a wad of chewing-baccy rolling over his stained teeth. 'Be all through by noon. There won't be nobody standin', not one. I guarantee it.'

Billet shifted his stance but held his narrow gaze tight on the street.

'Not yet,' grunted Prinz.

'Damn it, you keep on sayin' not yet! It's always not yet. And now look where we are,' quipped Murphy sardonically. 'We've lost Mouthy – and we don't know how; we ain't got a snitch of a hint as to who did it. And we've got a town spooked up and brewin' like bad hooch in a cracked glass.' He spat into the street. 'Time somebody paid. Time we did somethin'.'

Prinz gripped the lapels of his waistcoat. 'That's just what I was reckonin', Skeets,' said Prinz, his gaze flicking to left and right as if drawn on a string. 'And I figure for you bein' the one to do it.'

Murphy glared from the corners of his eyes. 'Why me? Why ain't we all for doin' whatever you got in mind?'

'T'ain't a job for three men,' answered Prinz, still scanning the street. 'Three would be noticed. One man might not.' He grinned quickly. 'You're that man.'

'To do what?'

'To get out there into them sands and find whoever it is playin' cat and mouse with us. Who gets to deliverin' a dead man's horse to my doorstep. Who gets to stealin' a coffin – and then fillin' it with one of my men.' Prinz's eyes steadied and settled on Murphy. 'If you find him, you kill him.'

'And if I don't?' asked Murphy.

'He'll mebbe kill you,' chipped Billet.

'That ain't funny,' grunted Murphy. 'How come we can't leave it to Mitchell and his boys? Hell, they'll be here soon. Gotta be. There'll be more guns among them than you can count. Them fellas'd mop up the scumbag in no time. I don't see as how–'

'You'll do like I say, Skeets, and you'll leave now,' ordered Prinz. 'You'll be back here by sundown. And I'll be waitin' to hear some good news from you. As for Mitchell and them ridin' with him, they ain't goin' to be in a mood to waste time messin' with some cheap smart-jack after the raid at North-forks. All they'll want from this town is what we're guaranteein' them – safety and a place to hole up 'til the heat's off. That's what we've promised; that's what we're bein' paid for, and very generously too. After that, we'll do what we like with Mission Rock and its folk.'

Prinz grinned and wiped a hand across his stubble to clear the sweat. 'Go earn some of that money, Skeets. We'll still be here when you get back waitin' patiently to hear the good news you'll be bringin'.'

Doc Cherry swallowed. His throat seemed to crack in the dry heat and the sudden throb of nerves that surged through him. He wanted desperately to turn, to see the form and true shape behind the shadow, but was rooted to the spot. Maybe for the better, he thought, swallowing again. One false move now and all hell might blaze from the barrel of a gun.

'Who ... who's there?' he croaked, struggling to find a voice for the words.

The shadow had halted. Silence. Nothing moved until Doc's mount tossed its head against a pestering fly and tack jangled loosely.

'You the Doc?' asked the voice almost casually. 'Doc Cherry?'

'That's me,' said Doc, half turning then thinking better of it. He risked a shading hand to his face to wipe away an irritating trickle of sweat. The sun burned; the heat thickened. 'And just who might you be, mister?' he managed behind more swallowing and sweating. 'I hadn't figured on encounterin' anybody–'

'I'd reckon for you bein' out here lookin' for me,' said the man. 'I'd be right, wouldn't I?'

'Well, I have been kind of wonderin' ... that is *we*, the folk back there in Mission Rock ... have been thinkin' that mebbe there was somebody, is somebody, who's takin' one hell of an interest in us. And we can't right now figure for why.' Doc croaked to an abrupt halt, waited, began again: 'That's assumin' you're the fella responsible for what's been happenin'.' His voice trailed away.

There was a long silence. Doc thought for

a moment that the man had faded away as mysteriously as he had appeared, but the shadow was still there, only fractionally short of its original growth across him.

'I know Mission Rock,' said the man at last. 'I know Sheriff Prinz and his men. I know why they're there and what they're waitin' for.'

'Well, I sure wish somebody would tell us, f'crissake!' flared Doc on a sudden surge of confidence and anger that raised the colour in his cheeks and the sweat on his brow. 'Goddamnit, there's been men murdered in cold blood back there. Shot and killed for no good reason. Women have been abused darn near at Prinz's whim. Nobody's safe, and it's gettin' worse, particularly since...' Doc hesitated. 'I was goin' to say since you brought that horse of Dusty Bing's back to town; not to mention the coffin and then the body... I tell you straight up, mister, we ain't got a lot goin' for us right now, and if things–'

'Sorry,' clipped the man, and fell silent again.

'Yeah, well, mebbe you are, but not half as much as them poor devils held in town without hope of gettin' free, leastways not without riskin' their very lives same as I've

101

done this mornin'. If Prinz gets to hear ... well, that's a risk I've already taken. Point is, who are you, what's your interest in Mission Rock, and just what is goin' on back there?'

Another long silence. Doc waited, tempted now in his new-found confidence to turn, face the man, see just who he was...

'Stay right where you are and just listen,' broke the voice again. 'Minutes, that's all it'll take. And then you ride for Mission Rock. Understand?'

Doc had thoughts already into words on the tip of his tongue, but this time he merely nodded, wiped the sweat clear of his eyes, and waited.

The man's shadow did not move as he began to speak.

CHAPTER FOURTEEN

Mission Rock drifted to noon. The heat grew deeper, stronger, the air thicker. A haze shimmered over the dirt. Silence seemed fixed, like something dumped for no place else to put it. Nobody moved until forced; most dozed and lazed, some slept, shutting out the misery of Prinz's threats and his stranglehold on the town and, not least, the deaths.

A handful of men and curious youths still gathered at Ma McCundrie's bar. The drinking was slow; the smoking lazy. Conversation was sparse, but occasionally one of the men would voice his anger, begin to sweat, wipe his face, and fall silent. The effort was too much.

Three bar-girls sidled about like lost moths. Their dresses looked depressed, their make-up wet and stale; they simply sat or strolled, lounged and idled slow steps to the 'wings to stare into the empty street. One of the younger men approached, but was not encouraged, and in turn was not disappointed. It was too hot for that sort of thing, anyhow.

Ma McCundrie creaked in her wheelchair, lit another cheroot and watched the bar and its customers through a tight, narrowed gaze. She wondered how deep into the sands Doc had ridden. She could guess well enough his mission, but it was risky, if Prinz got to hear... Or supposing Doc were to be seen by Skeets Murphy. He had left town at sunup. Why? And where was he heading? On the same quest as Doc?

A man came to his feet from a corner table, crossed to the bar and ordered a fresh bottle of whiskey.

'T'ain't right,' he growled, leaning heavily to one side as Mopps produced the bottle and polished up a clean glass. 'Fella shouldn't have to live like this. T'ain't natural. He should be free to come and go as he darn well pleases.' He closed one eye and glared at Mopps with the other. 'What do you reckon, old friend?' the man asked, his words beginning to slur. 'You reckon a fella should be free?'

'Guess you're right there.' The barman grinned and finished polishing the glass with a flourish.

'See,' said the man, 'old Mopps here agrees with me. Sure he does.' He turned to face the other customers. 'And I bet as how most of you do – in fact, all of you. Right?' He swayed, glared, winked and nodded. 'Oh, yes, you agree. I can see that. You bet I can see it.'

'Take it easy there, Joe,' called a man from the far side of the bar. ''Course we agree, but that don't mean–'

'But you're a whole sight too scared to do anythin' about it, eh?' the man slurred on, steadying his balance with a grip on the bar.

'Ain't that the case?'

'We ain't for gettin' ourselves blown clean apart on the whim of a scumbag gunslinger,' piped an old man, puffing on a cherrywood pipe. 'That's what we mean.'

The man at the bar swayed, took a heavy step, steadied, glared. 'Time we did somethin',' he began again, reaching for the bottle. 'Time we took charge, got our town back to where it was before before...' He gestured wildly, the bottle tight in his right hand. 'Before all this.' He took another step. 'I ain't scared none. Nossir, I ain't.' The words were tripping themselves up as they left his mouth. 'I ain't never been scared, not of nobody, not anytime, anywhere.'

Ma's wheelchair creaked menacingly. 'You've had enough there, Joe,' she pronounced through a curtain of smoke. 'Time you slept it off.' She propelled herself towards the bar. 'You just put that bottle aside like a good fella and go get some sleep. Bottle will still be here when you wake. You hear me Joe?'

The man swayed. A dribble of saliva slid in a gleaming line down his chin. He stared hard at Ma, his eyes swimming, blinking as they struggled to focus. The bottle hung heavy in his grip. 'Mebbe I'll do just that,

Ma,' he slurred, much to the surprise of the others. 'Yeah, mebbe I will.' He replaced the bottle on the bar. 'Got some business to attend to anyhow.'

The bar customers watched in silence as the man made his slow, uncertain way to the batwings. A girl stepped hurriedly aside, a weak, wan smile flickering on her lips as the man passed. A younger man held open a 'wing. 'See you later, eh, Joe?'

'Sure ... sure,' slurred the man, shuffling to the boardwalk. 'You bet to it, fella, you bet. Later... Got some business to look to.'

The man stepped carefully across the boardwalk, then slowly down the steps to the street. He shielded his eyes against the glaring stare of the sun, licked at a sudden bubbling of sweat across his lips, and turned towards the sheriffs office.

'Hell,' said the fellow at the 'wings, 'the darn fool's headin' for Prinz.'

The customers pushed back chairs, came to their feet and crossed to and then through the 'wings to the boardwalk. Ma creaked behind the throng, urging the girls to stay out of sight. Mopps followed in her wake, his hands buried in a glasscloth.

'What the hell's he doin'?' murmured a man in a board-brimmed hat.

'Crazy fool,' hissed another. The voices clamoured.

'He's mad.'

'Drunk more like.'

'Get himself killed.'

'We should do somethin'.'

A man called out, 'Hey, Joe, where you goin'?'

'You're goin' the wrong way, Joe,' echoed a second man from the front of the throng.

'Joe – you hearin' us?'

The man continued on his slow, uncertain way, his steps weakening, the sweat gleaming on his face. He halted some yards short of Prinz's office, swayed, shook himself to his full height, took two more steps and stopped again. His shadow spread long and lean ahead of him.

It was a full minute before a shape appeared at the sheriffs open door.

'Billet,' croaked a man, craning for a clearer view.

'Where's Prinz?' slurred Joe, squinting through a veil of sweat. 'I wanna see Prinz. Right now. I wanna tell him he ain't welcome in this town no more. You hear me there, fella?'

'I hear you,' said Billet, his thumbs hooked into his belt. 'Sheriff Prinz ain't available at this time. You wanna see him, you come back later when he ain't so busy.'

Joe steadied himself through a threatening sway. 'What's he so busy about he can't see a man on town business? You tell me that.'

Billet's eyes darkened.

'Well,' said Joe, 'you goin' to get Prinz out here, or do I have to step up there myself?'

Billet did not move. The crowd at Mc-Cundrie's saloon stood still and silent. Ma's wheelchair creaked. A bar-girl sniffed nervously.

'I ain't seein' no response from you, mister,' said Joe, leaning forward. 'Am I goin' to see you do somethin'?'

'Sure you are.' Billet grinned. 'How about this...' Joe would have seen the flash of Billet's hand to his Colt; he would have seen the draw, and in a moment of uncluttered clarity, have heard the blaze of the shot. Perhaps he felt the searing pain, but he was dead in the street dirt within seconds.

Billet stared towards the bar for a moment, shouted an order for the body to be removed, then turned on his heel and disappeared into the office.

The throng at the saloon drifted back to the bar, some murmuring among themselves, some simply silent, shuffling and locked into private thoughts. The bar-girls gathered like a clutch of nervous hens. Mopps took the bottle of whiskey from the bar and replaced it on the shelf.

Joe would not be coming back for it.

Elmer Puce had murmured the last rites over Joe within the hour. A handful of town men had been there to shovel dirt, mouth their own words of departure and sweat out their anger in stifled mumbling.

'No more,' said one. 'I ain't takin' no more.' The heavy-chested, broad-shoul-dered fellow brushed aside an embarrassing trickle of a tear, and sniffed loudly. 'If we don't get to doin' somethin' about all this today, what's left of it, then I'm goin' to–'

'End up dead, same as the soul you've just helped put to rest,' said George Wickham darkly, his eyes flicking to the heavy-chested man. He brushed lightly at dust on his waistcoat. 'We all feel the same, don't we? Anger, hatred ... sure, let's step out there and shoot the scum. Damnit, there's only two of 'em in that office. That ain't too much to ask of us, is it – to take 'em out like poppin' lead at perched birds? We can do that!' He grunted. 'Sounds easy, don't it? All of us against two of them. But who's got the guts? Who's got the guns?'

'Hold on there, George,' said Hank Stone, stepping closer over the dry, grainy sand of Boot Hill, 'there ain't a man here who wouldn't go along with your feelin's. We all would. Every last man. Ain't that so, fellas?'

Picky Layton nodded. Tinker Johnny murmured, 'Sure, sure...' The town men bowed their heads. One scratched the back of his neck. The man at his side startled settling flies and sent them buzzing.

'But you got to figure it, George,' the blacksmith went on, 'we ain't got no means of fightin' back, save with our bare hands. All we seem able to do is witness the killin's and bury the dead. And there don't seem much else of a prospect.'

'But there might be,' said a calm, careful voice at the back of the gathering.

CHAPTER FIFTEEN

'You mean there really is somebody out there and you've seen him?' Tinker Johnny peered deep into Doc's eyes. 'Hell, that must have been quite somethin'.'

'A mite scary to my reckonin',' said the undertaker, wiping a finger round the growing tightness of his shirt-collar.

'What did he say?' said Hank Stone.

'Yeah, let's hear the details,' urged George Wickham, glancing quickly over the faces of the men who'd left Boot Hill for the black-smith's stable to hear of Doc's journey to the sands. 'Before we do, one of us had best keep an eye on the street just in case Prinz or that murderin' deputy of his gets to bein' nosy.'

Doc waited until a look-out had been posted and he had the men's full attention.

'Like I said when I found you fellas back there on the hill,' he began, 'I didn't get to seein' the man's face full on. He wouldn't let me, but I saw all I needed to see and heard more than enough to make some sort of sense out of this mess and murder –

'specially after hearin' about what's happened here this afternoon.'

The gathering nodded and murmured.

'I didn't find the man, he found me,' Doc continued. 'He gave me no name, no hint of who he was or where he'd come from, but my guess would be he's definitely some manner of lawman, and he's been trailin' steadily this way for weeks, mebbe months. One thing's for certain, he sure as hell knows how to survive. Livin' out there in the sands can't be easy, but he does it and comes and goes like he was a shadow – as we know to well enough.'

Doc paused. His audience murmured again. An older man in a battered, dusty derby sporting a fancy tail-feather, said, 'Takes guts out there. I know, I've been there and done it.' He adjusted the hat to a jaunty angle. 'Fella's either a lawman or a gunslinger.'

Doc cleared his throat. 'Well, he weren't for sayin' right then, but he was clear enough on other matters.' The gathering settled to a tight, concentrated silence. 'Fact is, we're bein' used,' Doc went on. 'We're set up for bein' a hole into which a whole heap of ratbag scum is about to scurry any day now. The Mitchell gang.'

Mouths opened but found no voice. Jaws dropped. Wickham twirled his timepiece on a chain. Hank Stone leaned on a pitchfork. Tinker Johnny gulped and wiped an eye. Nobody moved. Few men blinked.

'Hell,' said Picky Layton. He waited a moment, then added, 'Oh, hell, that ain't good news.'

'It's bad,' echoed a tall, skinny fellow dressed in clothes that hung from him as if drooping from a peg. 'Bad as it comes.' He swallowed. 'Why?' he croaked. 'What we done to deserve them?'

'The Mitchell gang robbed the bank at Northforks some time back,' said Doc. 'Shot the town up as they usually do, and rode clear with a haul big enough to keep the whole nest of them in luxury for life. There's been a hunt on ever since; to the north, east and west – but not to the south. Nobody figured they'd ride south, seein' as how there ain't nothin' but sand.' He waited, raised his eyes carefully. 'And us,' he said darkly. 'There's us. Little old Mission Rock. We're goin' to be the hidin'-hole for the gang 'til the heat cools and they can clear the border in safety.' He raised an arm to hush the murmuring. 'And it's all courtesy of Sheriff Prinz.'

'How come?' asked Wickham, reversing the twirl of the timepiece. 'Where does he come to figure in this?'

'Seems like our Sheriff Prinz is a long-time associate of the Mitchell boys, which ain't surprisin', least-ways it ain't to me. I'd reckon him for straddlin' both sides of the law as it suits. It was our misfortune to have him fetch up here. Thinkin' is that havin' the gang hole up at Mission Rock was planned way back – doubtless on hefty payment and the promise of more to come, to Prinz and his sidekicks.'

'Mebbe it ain't too late to stop the Mitchells in their tracks,' said Hank.

'There'll be riders trailin' 'em fast, you can rest to that. But they won't hit the gang before the Mitchells hit us.'

'So what's the fella in the sands doin'?' asked the storekeeper, with another twirl of the timepiece. 'More to the point, what in tarnation does he reckon we can do?'

The men broke into a sudden babble of murmuring.

'Easy there, easy,' urged Wickham. 'Keep your voices down, fellas. We ain't for havin' company.'

Doc waited for a measure of silence before continuing. 'The man I saw said nothin' of

114

the part he's playin' in this. Not a word. He just knows what's happenin', and I believe him. Seems to me he's frustratin' Prinz best he can.'

'And makin' a darn good job of it,' interrupted Picky Layton. 'Hell, he's taken out Mouthy Kline, and Prinz is beginnin' to twitch some. Who knows what he might do next?'

'But he's only one man,' said the fellow in the derby. 'One man against the Mitchell gang. They'll ride in all of a dozen strong, mebbe stronger. He can't fight a battle like that, not alone he can't. And what can we do – the pick-handles and sticks boys of Mission Rock! Town'll run with blood 'til there ain't none of us standin'.'

The murmurings bubbled and babbled again. Wickham called for silence, but was forced to wait a full minute before inviting Doc to continue.

'What you say is right,' said Doc, 'there would be blood, and plenty of it, if all we had were pickhandles and sticks. That'd be madness.' He cleared a beading of sweat. 'But it ain't so,' he added quietly. 'We have guns, and if you'll listen up another minute, I'll tell you how we came by them. Then I'm leavin' to see Ma, to tell her what I've told you, and to put the finishin' touches to her plan of how we're goin' to prepare in the short time we have to fight back. So simmer down and listen up...'

'They're comin'. I can smell 'em. Damn it, I can darn near hear them!' Sheriff Prinz turned sharply on the boardwalk fronting his office and strode back to his desk where he poured two generous measures of whiskey. 'To us, Chine,' he said with a grin, raising his glass. 'I do believe we've pulled this off. Another few days, a week at most, and we'll be all through here and ridin' along of the Mitchells for the South. And, my friend, with money, real money, in our pockets. You'll want for nothin', mister, so drink up and pour another.'

Chine Billet finished his drink in a single gulp and replaced the glass on Prinz's desk. 'I don't smell nothin',' he sulked, strolling to the open door. 'And I don't hear nothin'. But I'm sure gettin' to fidget some over Skeets. It's close to dusk, sun's goin', and Skeets ain't showed. Where is he?'

'Skeets Murphy never did keep time save when he was chasin' some skittish whore. Then he could shift!' Prinz poured another drink. 'Don't worry, he'll be here, sandgrimed and stinkin' like a hog. But he'll be here. And I just hope he's bringin' some good news.'

Billet grunted and scanned the street. 'Town's quiet,' he said. 'Ain't a livin' soul to be seen.'

'Mebbe that's 'cus we keep killin' 'em off!' cracked Prinz. 'Hell, that was a fool of a drunk you took out earlier. Liquored-up to the eyeballs. If the Mitchells weren't so close I'd close that saloon down. Sure I would. 'Cept to us, o'course!'

'How can you be so certain about the Mitchells?' The deputy wiped a bandanna across his neck. 'I can't be that certain. I ain't no notion as to when they'll show. You sure you ain't just kiddin' yourself?'

'I don't never kid where the Mitchells are concerned. They're close, you can take my word on it. Real close. Now you step back here and share the rest of this bottle with me while we wait on Skeets.'

Billet shoved the bandanna into his belt and gave the street another scan. Still nobody about, still all quiet, solemn as Boot Hill. Dead as dirt. He grunted and went back to the office.

Skeets would be riding into darkness in under the hour.

CHAPTER SIXTEEN

Night came slowly to Mission Rock, like something in fear of being there. The shadows seemed deeper as if themselves in hiding, and the silence in the main street as George Wickham locked and bolted the store, doused the already dimmed lights and double-checked the doors, thickened. It might, he thought, have been listening.

And there was plenty to be heard.

It had been agreed by those assembled in Hank Stone's barn to hear Doc tell of his encounter in the sands and the guns Shamrock had risked her life for, that they would meet again in McCundrie's bar at nightfall. They would arrive carefully, one by one, or sometimes as a pair, a small group; a fellow might sneak in by the back door, another slip silently and unseen through the shadows, until all those who reckoned they could handle a gun – and were prepared to do so – were gathered.

'At no time should Prinz be aware of the meetin',' Wickham had pressed.

'And that's a whole sight easier said than done,' Elmer Puce had observed, dusting himself down of lingering Boot Hill dirt. 'I swear to God that sonofabitch sheriff has eyes in the back of his head.'

The men mumbled, muttered, fidgeted and sweated in the oppressive heat of the barn where even the slightest movement of a boot or a body raised a dancing glitter of dust. The single lantern's glow cast shadows, dark and deep, tall as columns, into the rafters. Men's eyes gleamed. Talk fell into silence.

'Let's leave it right there,' Hank Stone had insisted. 'You all know what's at stake. You've all heard what Doc has said. And, damn it, you know to the bone the implications if we don't get this right. And it's goin' to have to be a first-time right. No second chance, fellas. We're either with Mission Rock to the end, or we are the end...'

'Gatherin's at nightfall, Ma's place,' Wickham had added like an echoing afterthought.

'You want I should be there?' said Shamrock, slipping painfully into her best blue dress before checking out the drape in the full-length mirror and twirling to face Doc perched on the end of her unmade bed. 'T'ain't no problem.' She smiled. 'I can be there ... face 'em all ... tell it just like it was if that'll help.' The smile dimmed, the blue eyes faded to an aching grey. 'I ain't done all this – just like you see me – for nothin', have I, Doc?'

'Hey, now,' soothed Doc, coming to his feet to comfort the woman in his arms, 'would I – *me* of all people – be sayin' a thing like that? Hell, Shamrock, you've given more than we, this territory, mebbe this whole nation, will ever know for the survival of one small town.' He unfolded his arms, released her and stood back admiringly. 'You look great. And you know somethin', blue's my favourite colour. No kiddin'! Just great.'

He collected his hat and moved to the door. 'We'll be gathered in an hour,' he said quietly. 'Be there, my dear, be there – for all our sakes.'

They came, thought Doc, like mice. Watchful, careful, without so much as the creak of a boot, the hiss of a breath. No one spoke. Eyes glanced acknowledgement, then faded into the shadows. Someone lit a cheroot, another clinked a bottle to an unsteady glass. Ma McCundrie glared and monitored the arrivals like a schoolteacher counting in her charges.

'There ain't many, Doc,' she murmured. 'Fifteen at best. That goin' to be enough?'

Doc sighed and gazed, sometimes squinting through the darkness, over the faces of the town men gathered at the back of the saloon bar. 'Men have responsibilities,' he said quietly. 'Some are for family more than riskin' their own lives. Can't fault 'em for that, Ma. A man makes his own priorities, and I ain't critical of nobody. If fifteen's what we've got, fifteen will have to do it.'

Ma creaked her wheelchair and reached for the glass of brandy on the table facing her. 'Ain't one of 'em looks to be a gunman. How long since any of 'em handled a piece, let alone fired one?'

'That,' said Doc, 'is somethin' we're goin' to have to find out.' He stepped from Ma's side, nodded to George Wickham, checked with Mopps standing look-out at the batwings, then turned to face the assembled town men.

'Thanks for bein' here,' he began, clearing a trickle of sweat from his brow. 'Ain't no point in a speech, so here's the drift of it for them still prepared to take up a gun in defence of our town.'

'Survival as most of us see it, Doc,' said a voice from the lantern-lit shadows.

'Guess you're right,' said Doc. 'Survival it is.'

Ma creaked her chair again for attention. 'There's an old cellar right under where you're sittin'.' She glared, her grey eyes darting across the faces turned to her. 'A secret place, somewhere most of you didn't know to and had no good reason to neither.'

'That's true, Ma.' Picky Layton nodded, fixing his hands flat to his knees. 'But how come?' he added, frowning.

'T'ain't of no consequence,' said Ma, brushing Picky's comments aside. 'Point is, it's there – and right now full of guns and enough ammunition to feed 'em 'til we're all through and done.'

A burst of murmuring swept among the men. An old man clamped an unlit pipe between his four good teeth and sucked on it. A tall, sallow-faced fellow lifted his hat and scratched through his hair as if under attack by lice; another slapped his thigh and raised his eyes; a youth swallowed, licked his lips and felt his gut run suddenly cold. Hank Stone sighed and folded his arms. Elmer Puce mouthed a prayer. Tinker Johnny shuddered and tried not to show it.

A voice cut through the muted babble. 'That's all very well, Ma, but how we goin' to set about usin' 'em? I mean, there ain't no good goin' to come of just loosin' them off like we were poppin' at crop crows, is there? We gotta have a plan, f'cris'sake. Hell, there might be the whole of the Mitchell scum here by sundown tomorrow. And what about that fella prowlin' about out there in the sands? We might be facin' a whole lot more than Prinz. We might–'

'Listen up, all of you.'

The cutting edge to Shamrock's words sliced through the bar like a blade. The men turned to face her where she stood at the foot of the stairs, one hand on the banister rail, the other loose in the drape of her blue dress. Their eyes scanned over the deep bruising across her neck and shoulders, saw the still raw cuts and grazing across her cheeks, the swollen right eye, the painful lift and fall of her breasts as she struggled to steady her breathing.

'I don't want no questions.' She smiled weakly. 'I ain't givin' no explanations as to how this all came about – Doc and Ma will do that – I'm just askin' all of you, every last one, to take a gun and do as Doc and Mr

Wickham here tell you. Take it, then wait 'til you get your orders.' She steadied herself against the rail, rallied the smile, and murmured: 'Do it for Mission Rock; do it for me, but most of all do it for yourselves.'

Not a man stirred. No one spoke. Nothing moved in the deep, clinging heat of that night as Shamrock smiled again, turned and made her slow, graceful way back to her room

But there were some there whose eyes were unashamedly wet.

It was after midnight when Doc Cherry shuffled the papers littering his desk into a neat handful, locked them away in a side drawer, pocketed the key and yawned through a weary stretch.

All done, he decided, leastways as far as he could take matters for the time being. The town had gained a few more hours at best, he reflected, shuddering tired limbs through the last of the yawn, but now it was ready, no doubt of that; ready as it would ever be, given the number of guns it could summon into willing hands.

George Wickham had led the town men, one by one, into the hidden cellar beneath the bar until every man had his weapon and the bullets to arm it. The minutes, for Doc, had ticked by like hours as his fear of Prinz putting in an appearance had deepened. But Mopps had remained silent and unmoving at the batwings. Prinz had stayed tight in his office with Chine Billet along of him. But just where, Tinker Johnny had whispered in Doc's ear, was Skeets Murphy? Doc had merely shrugged and heaved a sigh of relief as the trap-door to the cellar had locked into place again and the last man had been armed.

'Keep them guns safe and don't do nothin' 'til you hear from either me or Doc,' the storekeeper had ordered. He had grinned. 'Take yourselves a drink, natural as ever, and then shift, quiet as mice...'

Doc yawned again, blinked twice as he forced his eyes open and stood perfectly still at the sound of a soft tap at his front door.

'Who in the name of tarnation at this hour...' he murmured, crossing to the door and opening it.

He stared into the sweat-gleaming face of Tinker. 'Skeets ain't back from the sands,' he hissed, glancing quickly behind him. 'I've just been nosin' round the sheriffs office. There ain't nobody there save Prinz and Billet, and no mount hitched up neither. So what's happened to Murphy? He still out there, or is he...?' He hesitated, swallowed and broke into a fresh lathering of sweat. 'Could we get so lucky... Could he be dead?'

CHAPTER SEVENTEEN

It was the smell of dust that woke Hank Stone. A thin, distant, approaching aroma that sweetened the air at this time of day with the sun not yet clear of the far horizon. A smell that lingered, warning of hoofs turning dirt to send it drifting through already warm summer air, catching at the softest dawn breeze.

But it was still some minutes before Hank actually opened his eyes, blinked, sniffed, swallowed on a parched throat and struggled to sit upright on a nest of baled straw in the livery barn.

A horse snorted; a hoof stamped. 'Easy, fellas, easy,' he murmured, coming to his feet to glance quickly over the stabled mounts. 'I hear you, I hear you.'

He crossed slowly to the half-open barn door, pushed it on the full swing of its hinges and shaded his eyes against the gathering first-light glare. Morning was up and kicking. The sort of morning he had seen hundreds of times before, except that this particular one carried the shape of a dust cloud and the sound of oncoming riders.

And they were in a hurry.

Tinker Johnny had not even bothered to sleep. He had been a whole sight too busy keeping a watch on Prinz, his deputy Chine Billet, and the slightest movement in and around the sheriff's office.

Something, he had decided long since, after leaving Doc's place, was not right. Skeets Murphy had not shown – and there was still neither sight nor sound of him. So where was he: still out there in the sands, or maybe riding on? Perhaps he had quit, told Prinz he was no longer into the plan to help Mitchell and his gang. Or perhaps – and this was the chilling doubt that was gnawing at Tinker's thoughts – he had left town to greet Mitchell and guide him into Mission Rock.

And then, of course, there was the question of the stranger Doc had met. Supposing he...

It was then that Tinker's nostrils had twitched and he had smelled the approaching dust.

Ma McCundrie had been dreaming most of that night. She had dreamed she was out of her wicker wheelchair, her limbs alive and strong, her hair loose as she rode the plains like the wind. And then she had woken, cursed, lit a cheroot and creaked her chair to the bottle of brandy set on her private table.

No good ever came of dreams, she had resolved once again. It was best to sleep on, or stay wide awake, watch the night, the first hint of light and smell the new day.

But today she smelled the dust of riders. Fast riders approaching across the sands. And it was no dream.

Picky Layton had also dreamed that night, just as he did most nights, and once again his dreams had been of the pretty brunette in the blue dress. But on this night the images had been fleeting and sometimes jumbled: the girl, the dress, her face, and then, without warning, Prinz, his sidekicks, the voices of the men at the meeting in the saloon, the pitch darkness of the cellar, a swaying lantern, the gleam of guns ... and back to Prinz seated in the barber's chair, demanding a shave.

Picky had woken in a sweat, the gun handed to him by Wickham, under his pillow. It had been some minutes before he slid his feet to the floor, left the bed and stepped unsteadily to the open window overlooking the street.

The room above the shop afforded a long view, beyond the livery to where the sands began their sweep from the last of the town to the far horizon. At this hour, with the night still fading and the dawn not yet full, there was little to be seen save the shadows and the blurred edges of shapes. But when Picky took a deep breath and smelled freshly disturbed dust and then heard the distant rumbling of what might have been a gathering storm but was unmistakably the drone of pounding hoofs, he knew this was going to be no ordinary day.

He was only minutes behind Doc Cherry when he left the shop and headed for the livery. It was there, he figured, that the riders would ease up and reckon they had reached safety. Here too that Mission Rock would learn its fate.

Seconds behind Picky on that morning were Sheriff Prinz and Chine Billet, also heading for the livery. But they carried loaded guns, and Prinz was smiling.

The throng of town men, a handful of women and curious, wide-eyed youngsters, gathered quickly on the street even at that hour, though many men had not slept and most only fitfully. Shamrock and the bar girls huddled in their wraps and watched from the saloon windows as Mission Rock stirred into silent life. Few spoke, save in hushed murmurings and muttered comments.

Some men had considered carrying the newly issued weapons hidden in their shirts, but thought better of it. Supposing somebody got spooked or careless; supposing a gun went off... Hell, that would turn the taps on a blood-bath. No, they would wait for orders as instructed.

Ma McCundrie wheeled herself on to the saloon veranda, a bottle of brandy and three cheroots settled to hand in the folds of her skirts. George Wickham ensured that the doors to the store, back and front, were secure and locked. Some folk took to hiding treasured belongings and secreting their savings about them. 'Can't be too careful,' an old-timer had advised, pocketing all the tobacco and pipes he had. 'Me, I ain't got nothin' worth the takin', so whoever's out there, whoever's beatin' all hell's dirt to get here, is welcome to what I have – if he don't mind smokin' on another man's pipe!'

Doc Cherry, Wickham, Elmer Puce, Tinker Johnny and Picky Layton joined Hank at the livery and stood in a silent line, their eyes fixed on the sands, the approaching dust cloud and the lifting light that revealed more by the minute.

'Quite a crowd,' murmured Hank. 'Goin' to keep me busy.'

'For no pay,' said Layton. 'Types like them don't ever pay, not even when they've got it; a whole hoard of it if that's the Mitchell gang we got comin'.'

'It's them sure enough,' grunted Elmer. 'I just hope they ain't reckonin' on a killin'-spree. There just ain't the timber for decent burials.'

The men fell silent; few in the street behind them made any movement or sound. Only the gathering beat of hoofs swelled and deepened until it seemed to fill the morning and hold the townsfolk in a trance.

It was the bellowing voice of Sheriff Prinz that broke the moment.

'You stay nice and quiet, all of you,' he shouted, striding down the middle of the street, gesturing to left and right with a wave of the Winchester in his grip. 'No sounds, no comin' and goin'. Them fellas ridin' in right now are here for as long as it suits. Understand? You make 'em real welcome and you won't get hurt. You do the other thing and you sure as hell will, 'til it hurts. I make myself clear?'

He halted, gazed round him, waited for Chine Billet to join him, then strode on towards the livery, the faces ranged along the boardwalks watching him in silence.

Prinz halted again at McCundrie's saloon and fixed Ma with a fish-eyed stare as the full morning light broke across his dark, stubbled face. 'You get that bar open, Ma, minute my friends hit town,' he ordered, a bubbling of sweat gleaming on his cheeks. 'Boys'll be real parched after their ride. And do somethin' with them girls, fcris'sake. They look like worn sheets! Get 'em dressed proper, smarten 'em up.'

Ma's only response from the wicker chair was to creak it indignantly and blow a thin line of smoke from her glowing cheroot.

Prinz snorted and strode on. 'And what's all this?' he growled as he reached the line of men at the livery. 'A reception committee? You promoted yourselves to town fathers or something'?' He snorted and grinned. 'Beginnin' to realize which side of the bed's for sleepin' on, eh? Comin' to your senses. Well, I'm glad to see it, 'cus I'll tell you somethin', them boys ridin' in there won't be for takin' no messin' from nobody. So you just keep your noses clean for everybody's sake.'

Prinz shielded his eyes against the glare of the brightening light. Billet shouldered his rifle and flicked his gaze watchfully over the faces turned to the sands. He trusted no one. It was just second nature.

'Notice somethin'?' whispered Tinker Johnny at Doc's side. Doc glanced at him from the corner of his eyes. Tinker's eyes sparkled. 'Skeets Murphy is still missin',' he hissed, 'and my guess would be–'

But by then the pounding of the hoofs drowned his words.

CHAPTER EIGHTEEN

They came into view like an advancing army; at first no more than blurred, heat-hazed shapes, then growing clearer as the light strengthened and the day dawned.

Soon, for those watching, still silent and unmoving, the shapes darkened until squinting eyes could make out legs and hoofs, lathered bodies, boots and stirrups, hands and arms and then faces, wet and streaming sweat. And at last, through the cloud and dust and above the snorts of anxious mounts, the ceaseless jangle of tack and creaking leather, the folk of Mission Rock saw eyes, at least twenty pairs of them, tight and narrowed on their two-bit, back-of-the-heap town.

'Lord above, they even smell like death,' murmured Doc.

The town men waited another full two minutes for the leading rider to draw the force to a halt in a swirling mass of dust and dirt.

'Rogan!' shouted Prinz, striding to greet the riders. 'Rogan Mitchell! Goddamn it, I been waitin' on this for more time than I can recall. How are you, Rogan? How's the boys? Some heist you pulled there back at Northforks, eh? You bet to it. Why, I'd wager right now that folk across this whole territory, length and breadth of it, are reckonin' it straight into history. Like I've been tellin' Chine here–'

Rogan Mitchell, tall and straight in the saddle, the brim of his black hat pulled low to his brow, darkening the pitted, sun-burned, wind-whipped glow of his face, spat a long fount of spittle to the dirt, wiped a hand across his mouth and glared into Prinz's eyes.

'This town clear like you promised?' he grated, the words grinding from his mouth as if mixed with sand. He coughed, spat again, slid gnarled fingers to a hold on the bandanna at his neck and wiped it across his parched lips.

'It'd better be,' he went on. 'My boys are fair ridden-through. Ain't that so, fellas?' The riders ranged behind him mouthed their agreement, some scratching armpits, heads, thighs, others reaching for canteens, slopping water over mouths, lips and neck.

They seemed, thought Doc, to be relieved to be at a destination, anxious for something that had neither the taste nor feel of sand. And tired. Hell, were they tired.

'No worries, Rogan, no worries at all.' Prinz smiled stiffening and preening himself, flicking at a darker fleck of dust among the smear of it across his waistcoat. 'Town's tight, under *my* control. You ain't got no fears here, old friend. There's a mercantile – under the charge of Wickham here – and stocked with just about anythin' you could be wishin' for. Yessir! And no payment required for your needs, nor expected, just as you'd have wanted, Rogan. Ain't that so, Wickham? Step up and tell the man.'

George Wickham fumed until the colour rose in his cheeks like a sunrise and sweat beaded on his brow. Doc prompted him with a nudge. The others looked on anxiously. The storekeeper took a deep breath, snorted, tensed his muscles and broke from the gathering of town men. 'I'm Wickham,' he snapped, his stare fixed on Mitchell's face. 'George Wickham to be precise, *Mr Wickham* to you and your boys. And Wickham's store don't offer no credit, save to those I deem fit to receive it. Them's my rules. Pay your way, or get out!'

Mitchell spat another long line of spittle, wiped his mouth and gestured Prinz clear of launching a blow at Wickham. 'A man after my own heart.' He beamed. 'Mr storekeeper here conducts his business accordin' to his rules. Same as me, eh, boys? We work to rules, don't we?' The riders muttered their agreement. 'So there'll be no helpin' yourselves at Wickham's store. You hear me?' He leaned forward in the saddle to glare at Prinz. 'So what else you got lined up, Sheriff? Whiskey – quality whiskey? I don't drink no cheap hooch. And girls. My boys are in sore need of girls. Lots of 'em. Good, clean girls. Pretty as spring and dressed for summer.' He smiled a long, slow-moving smile that seemed to spread his lips like mud. 'You've got that organized, Mr Prinz?'

'You can bet to that.' Prinz swelled. 'Ma McCundrie's saloon. Straight down the street. And they're waitin' on you – don't doubt it. Girls as fresh as mornin' daisies. You won't be disappointed, Rogan, that I can vouch for personally.' He wiped heavy sweat from his face. 'And there's beds, clean sheets, food ... barberin' at Picky Layton's place, and we've even got a doctor here. Doc Cherry, best in the territory.' He wiped his face again. 'You ain't to be wantin' for nothin' in Mission Rock, Rogan. You just name it and we've got it – and if we ain't, we'll sure as hell get it.'

Prinz nodded to himself, smiled, hooked his thumbs in his belt and beckoned for Chine Billet to step to his side. 'Chine here will agree. You tell 'em, Chine, just lay it out–'

'Where's Murphy?' growled Mitchell. 'I don't see him along of you, Sheriff. And I don't see Mouthy Kline neither. Where are they? Don't tell me they've pulled out on us.'

The sweat began to bubble on Prinz's face. 'No, no, they ain't pulled out, nothin' like it.' His smile weakened. He shrugged his shoulders uncomfortably, glanced anxiously back to the town men, and adjusted his tightening hat with a flourish. 'Fact is, we've got some annoyin' local trouble. Nothin' we can't handle, you understand. Just a pesky fly buzzin' where it ain't wanted. But don't you fret none, Rogan, me and Chine–'

Mitchell's eyes narrowed. 'How pesky?'

'I'll tell you,' said Picky Layton, pushing himself clear of the line of men. 'I'll tell you exactly.'

Chine Billet reached to grab the barber.

Prinz glared, sweat pouring down his florid cheeks. Doc Cherry stumbled over feet to restrain Picky, but was already a step behind Wickham who succeeded in laying a hand on Layton's shoulder.

'Easy there, fella, easy,' George soothed, urging the other town men to stay back. 'We don't know nothin' as will serve any purpose right now.'

'But that's the whole point, we *do* know,' said Picky, shrugging off Wickham's hold. 'We do know there's somebody out there, has been for days. We know he brought Dusty's mount in, we know he stole that coffin from Elmer's yard, and we know, 'cus we seen it with our own eyes right there in the street, the night the stranger killed Mouthy Kline and dumped his body in that self-same coffin. Now ain't that so, folk?' His face gleamed in the bright morning light as he swung round to the town men at the livery and then lifted his gaze to the gathering in the street. 'I'm right, aren't I?' he called. 'We all know to it.' He caught his breath, gulped, blinked and ran his sweating hands down his pants. 'And Doc here's seen him. Ain't that so, Doc? You tell 'em.'

Doc Cherry sighed and was once again a step behind the storekeeper as he reached to pull Picky back to the line of men.

Prinz fumed, his gaze fixed on Rogan Mitchell's face. Chine Billet brandished a Winchester in a wide, swinging arc. No one moved. No one spoke. Mitchell stared at Picky Layton. The dusty, trail-stained riders sweated.

'Now let's get this straight right now,' said Wickham, with a bristling of his jacket to signify his civic importance. 'It's true.' He grinned weakly. 'We do have a stranger hereabouts, but, hell, we get drifters, legless no-hopers drowned in booze all the time; folk who just come from nowhere and ain't goin' no place particular. They're twenty to a cent any time, any day of the week. But that don't mean to say–'

'Shut it, the lot of you!' spat Mitchell, leaning across his mount's neck to stare directly into Wickham's eyes. 'I've heard enough of this.' The stare deepened and blackened to a needle-sharp glare. 'I want some facts, real facts. And damn the hide of any fella here who ain't prepared to speak the truth of what he knows and what he's seen.' The slide of his lips to a sickening smile oozed through a dribbling of sweat from the corners of his mouth. 'Understand? You all hearin' me?'

Silence. Mission Rock and its gathered

folk simply stared, but did not move.

'Good,' grinned Mitchell, leaning back to sit fully upright in the saddle. 'Good, real good. Nice town you've got here.' His lips sank to a miserable twist as he gestured with his right arm for three of his men to ease their mounts forward. 'My best boys,' he announced, his eyes sparkling. 'Dead certain shots, but in need of some activity of a refreshing nature.'

The assembled town folk – those at the livery, those in the street – heard the slam of Winchesters primed and ready for action. They saw Mitchell's chosen trio raise their weapons, and then they heard the roar of shots repeated again and again.

Until the blood was staining that fresh morning light.

CHAPTER NINETEEN

Chine Billet fell as if his legs had been cut from under him. His eyes widened in a stare of disbelief. His mouth opened but never closed as the thickening darkness swept over him.

Prinz had taken only a half-step when he too stared, a single sound breaking across his lips, raised his arms as if to protect himself but was thrown back under the hail of fire that ceased almost as instantly as it had begun.

Mitchell sat stony-faced, not a muscle twitching, not an eyelid blinking, his expression suddenly grey and distant.

The town folk stood in silence, their gazes fixed on the face of the new terror that had ridden in.

'Careless,' said Mitchell at last. 'They got careless. Should've taken care of that stranger. I don't like strangers.' His gaze settled on Doc. 'Me and you are goin' to talk. I want to hear exactly who you met, when and where and what was said. In detail. Understand?'

'There's not much–' began Doc.

Mitchell snapped the reins to his mount through his fingers. 'Not here. You follow me.' He turned to his three marksmen. 'Get the street clear. I don't want to see no more gawpin' faces. Then get the boys settled.' He turned to the town men at the livery.

'Seein' as you fellas look to be some sort of reception committee, you follow along of Doc here.' He snapped the reins again. 'And get them bodies shifted. Place is beginnin' to smell.'

'Nightmare. It's a nightmare. There ain't no other word for it.' Tinker Johnny scuffed his boots, missed his step and reached for George Wickham's arm as the town men – now dubbed the reception committee by Mitchell – made their slow way from the livery to the street. 'Damn it,' added Tinker, 'did you see all that? 'Course you did. Shot that scumbag Billet and that crazed sheriff we somehow got roped with clean through. I ain't never seen a killin' like it. Most folk here ain't neither. Ask 'em. Hell, all that blood flyin' and splatterin'–'

'Just simmer down there, fella,' urged the storekeeper, patting the man's arm but with his gaze still on Mitchell up ahead, his trio of henchmen at his side, the rest following, rifles drawn, stares watchful and mean as they headed for the street. 'Picky shouldn't have spoken like he did, but it's done and we're sure as day all through with Sheriff Prinz and his murderin' rats.' Wickham's eyes narrowed. 'Though quite what we got in their place ain't for speakin' of right now...'

The same thought had occurred to Doc,

though he had reckoned himself a mite too close to the notorious Mitchell to pursue the matter. Facts were that Prinz was no more; his ruthless rule had ended for him and Chine Billet in the spit and snarl of gunfire.

But what of Skeets Murphy? What of the guns now held by the town men? And what, in hell's name, of any plan to use them? There was Mitchell himself and at least twenty blood-soaked, free-killing men along of him, a force that could smother Mission Rock – and suffocate it any time it chose – out of sight, off the map, dead and buried for all time. Unless...

'I'll make the sheriff's office my place of residence,' said Mitchell, grinning. 'Somewhere here kind of private, eh, Doc? And official, seein' as I'm now... Well, shall we say, in charge?' He spat carefully ahead of Doc's next step, snapped the reins through his fingers and broadened the grin to a leering smile. 'And that's where we'll talk, Doc. Just you and me. How about that?'

George Wickham paced carefully the length of his store, halted to straighten a pile of blankets, move a box into line with its neighbour, turned and paced back again to the door where Elmer Puce watched the empty street.

'Shudder to reckon what them scumbag sidekicks of Mitchell's are doin' in Ma's place,' murmured the undertaker as Wickham came to his side. 'A nightmare, like Tinker said, 'specially for them girls.' He released the sweaty tightness of his black hat. 'A sight more than even Ma can handle.'

Wickham consulted his timepiece. 'How long now?' He frowned, staring at the watch-face as if expectin' it to answer. 'How long's Doc been holed up with Mitchell?'

'Too long for Doc's comfort, I'll wager,' said Elmer, shifting his gaze to the sheriffs office where the door remained closed and the window dark in the shade of the veranda. 'Mitchell won't get much out of Doc, that's for sure.'

Wickham returned his timepiece to his pocket. 'T'ain't the point, though, is it? Longer Doc's in there, the longer it's goin' to take to get ourselves organized.' He wiped his face with a clean bandanna. 'Damnit, we should be makin' a move, strikin' now while we've got the chance. Gettin' shut of Prinz and Billet is one thing, but waitin' on Mitchell gettin' his own grip on the town ain't servin' no purpose at all.'

'Fryin'-pan to fire, as they say,' said Elmer, squinting into the still glaring light of the day.

'Exactly that. Only a matter of time before Mitchell and them rats ridin' along of him are rulin' the roost here – and probably a deal harsher than Prinz ever did. Hell, they could be here for days, weeks even. And they ain't goin' to leave a deal in the way of witnesses when they do pull out, are they? They'll be treatin' us same as they served Prinz.'

Elmer rubbed his chin. 'Mebbe we should get some of the town boys together right now,' he mused. 'Another hour and them gunslingers whoopin' it up at Ma's are goin' to be boozed through to their skulls. What with the drink and the attractions of the girls, they might–'

'Hold it,' said Wickham urgently. 'Some-thin's happenin' top end of the street by the livery.'

The two men shaded their eyes to focus on the blurred, shimmering shape of a lone rider making a slow, almost mournful way from the sands to where Hank Stone, stripped to the waist, hammer in hand, waited at the smoking forge.

'Two bits to a coffin-lid if that don't look

146

to be the spittin' image of Skeets Murphy trailin' in there,' said Elmer.

The storekeeper grunted and concentrated his gaze. 'You're right,' he muttered. 'And he don't look none too healthy neither.'

Skeets Murphy had been dead some hours. He had been shot through the chest by a high-powered rifle ranged at maximum distance in a marksman's hands. 'Clean and simple as it gets,' had been Doc's verdict when the body had been unroped from its supported position in the saddle. 'And whoever did the shootin' knew full well the horse would head for town instinctively.'

'The stranger in the sands,' someone had murmured in the gathering of town men who had quickly filled the street again.

'Got to be,' added another.

'Same fella as took out Mouthy Kline,' said a third. The men muttered and murmured among themselves, some pressing forward for a closer look at the body. Some spat in contempt to the memory of his arrogant bullying; some merely thrust their hands into deep pockets and did no more than stare.

One man, a thick-chested fellow with the brim of his hat pulled as low as it would stretch, glanced quickly round him, disregarding Mitchell and his boys, and voiced the thoughts of most of those gathered there. 'I'd reckon for our stranger bein' one helluva fella, not to mention some of a shot, eh?' The town men shifted, shuffled, nodded and murmured. 'Got a real sense of the bizarre too. Body in a stolen coffin, then another roped upright to his horse. Hell, makes you wonder what he's goin' to come up with next time.'

'There ain't goin' to be a next time,' growled Mitchell, elbowing his way through the throng, two sidekicks flanking him, Doc trailing in his wake. 'There ain't no loss in Skeets Murphy,' he said, staring at the stiffening body. 'No loss at all. Saved me the bother of shootin' him myself.'

He spat, lifted his eyes and glared. 'I've listened to what Doc here's got to say of the man he met in the sands, and I believe him. But whoever it is playin' smart dog out there ain't for breathin' much longer. Too right he ain't. We'll take care of him. Startin' right now.'

Mitchell signalled to his men assembled in front of the saloon. 'A dozen of the boys will ride out, find the scumbag and bring him in alive.' He grinned. 'Then we'll have ourselves a hangin'. One of them slow, lingerin' hangin's where a fella gets to chokin' and kickin' and chokin' some more... Yeah, one of them.' He signalled again. 'Get to it, boys!'

It was not until Mitchell's men had saddled up, swung their mounts through a dustcloud and headed down the street to where the sands sprawled like a scorched wasteland, that Shamrock succeeded in easing her way through the gathered knots of town men to Doc's side.

'Round up the fellas,' she said quietly, watching Mitchell make his slow way back to the sheriff's office. 'Gather at the saloon. Soon as you can.' Her eyes gleamed in her anxious glance. 'And make sure they're carryin' guns. Time's come.'

CHAPTER TWENTY

The heat was still stiff, the sun-glare dazzling when Doc made his last call and headed back to the main street and the saloon.

He had moved quickly and silently from

man to man among those armed from the cache of guns. A few whispered words had been enough for the listener to nod and begin to make a carefully paced way to McCundrie's bar.

'Go easy. Don't draw attention to yourself. Them Mitchell scum ain't for bein' fussed who they kill or when,' Doc had urged.

Now, as he made his own watchful way along the boardwalks, his eyes tightened on the positioning of Mitchell's men. Of the twenty who had ridden in behind their leader, twelve had left again for the sands in search of the 'pesky' stranger.

Mitchell had positioned two of the remaining eight outside his headquarters at the sheriffs office; six had been ordered to patrol the town, moving sometimes in pairs, sometimes singly, from one end of the street to the other.

They strolled, paused, idled. They would reach an alley between buildings, and probe it; they looked over the goods at Wickham's store, dallied over Picky Layton's limited range of aftershaves, ran their thumbs across his razors, moved on to the saloon where a pair of them helped themselves to a bottle of whiskey, fondled the bar-girls, and strolled away. Ma simply seethed without making a sound.

Doc sank back to the deepest of the shadows. It might look almost too simple, he thought, to take out at least two if not more of the gunslingers right now. A steady hand, a carefully aimed shot... One down. But never that easy, he grunted, wiping a bandanna over his face as he continued his way to the saloon. The retribution would be bloody and as vicious as Rogan Mitchell could devise. And he had a wide repertoire, Doc was sure. No, better to wait maybe another hour, maybe two. Who cared? Mission Rock had been waiting for what seemed to many a lifetime already.

He reached the bar, pushed open the 'wings and stepped inside.

It was the silence that gripped, a wasteland of sound where no one moved and stood frozen in time. Familiar faces stared, but seemed to be strangers. The men, like the town, waited in the now softening afternoon light, some with untouched drinks, others standing anxiously, shifting foot to foot, careful not to make a sound. Some smoked; one man stood guard at the window with the clearest view of the sheriff's office. He nodded as Doc appeared.

Ma was the first to speak. 'We all here?'

she asked, creaking restlessly in her wheel-chair.

'Give it ten minutes,' said Doc, moving to the bar, where Mopps poured him a generous measure.

'We ain't got more,' said Elmer Puce, fidgeting at a corner table. 'Them others could be back from the sands any minute. And who's to say them scum out there aren't gettin' thirsty. They could step–'

'Give it a rest, Elmer,' snapped Wickham, joining Doc at the bar. 'We've all got eyes. We all know what *might* happen. So far, it ain't.'

Shamrock closed the door quietly to the back room, stepped into the dimming light and gazed over the faces of the town men. 'Here's the plan,' she began. She fixed her hands at her waist. 'And once started there ain't no goin' back...'

It was a sour-faced, sulk of a man, one of Mitchell's men patrolling the street, who paused in his steady pacing and stood listening as if the hot early-evening silence had suddenly spoken.

Something was different, not as it had been. His dark hooded eyes scanned the boardwalks, buildings, the soft spiral of smoke at the livery forge; left to right, left again, and then, without the man needing to move his head, in closer detail.

The street was empty. No one was coming or going, waiting or lounging. The man spat where he stood. A fly buzzed angrily. His gaze narrowed on the saloon. There were townfolk in there, he had seen them go in, heard and watched the creak of the 'wings. But no one had come out. And the place was all quiet. Too darned quiet.

He took a firmer grip on his Winchester and crossed the street with easy, unhurried steps. The hooded eyes worked frantically across the saloon windows, the batwings, and the shadowy gloom beyond them. No faces to be seen. No shapes. And still no sounds.

He halted at the three steps to the boardwalk and stared. He spat again, flexed the rifle in his grip and, without another glance at the saloon, turned and stepped out briskly to the sheriff's office, summoning the others on patrol to follow him.

'He's figured it,' murmured Picky Layton in Doc's ear. 'He knows we're here.'

'Mebbe,' said Doc, stepping closer to the window to follow the sour-faced man's steps to the office. 'But that's no bad thing.

Sooner we're into this and squared up, the better.'

'It'll be a blood-bath,' muttered Elmer Puce to himself. 'I ain't goin' to cope. There ain't goin' to be nothin' like enough timber.'

'Keep your thoughts to yourself, Elmer,' said Wickham, wiping the sweat from his face.

Elmer grunted, licked frantically at his pencil and slumped into a thoughtful gloom. The town men moved carefully round the bar, craning to squint into the street.

'Won't take Mitchell's men long to make a move,' said a man at the back of the group. The others craned again. 'Any sign yet?' piped a voice.

Shamrock turned her back on the street and faced the men.

'Let's get organized here,' she gestured, making her way to the bar. 'Three men at each window. Two at the 'wings. Six of you get upstairs, take up your positions in the rooms.' She looked at Ma. 'Ma, you stay close to me. No trundling around. Right?' Ma nodded and settled the Colt in her lap within easy reach of her grip.

'You girls stay low,' Shamrock ordered as the bar girls gathered in a still tighter clutch in the shadows. 'There's goin' to be some

154

lead flyin' fast and furious. Don't get in its path.'

She turned to Doc, her gaze softening. 'Guess you'll go where you're needed, Doc,' she said quietly.

Doc smiled softly. 'As ever,' he murmured. 'You watch out for yourself, you hear?'

Shamrock tossed her hair, flickered a smile, touched Doc's arm and turned away to watch the men taking up position.

Elmer Puce sank a measure of whiskey in one gulp. Tinker Johnny had closed his eyes in silent prayer. Hank Stone, positioned at the 'wings, stared into the street as if watching his thoughts translate to vivid pictures among the stiffening shadows as dusk gathered. Picky Layton watched the pretty girl he so desperately wanted to talk to somewhere private and alone. Would he live long enough to get the chance, he wondered? Ma creaked her wheelchair, lit a cheroot and scowled darkly.

'Here they come,' said Wickham.

The bar fell silent and unmoving.

Mitchell's men moved from the boardwalk fronting the sheriffs office to the street like stirred lizards seeking cover. They went singly, some to the far side, some staying opposite, and disappeared almost instantly into the alleys between buildings and the sudden spread of the early dusk.

Doc Cherry watched anxiously from a window in the bar, George Wickham at his shoulder. 'Can't see any of 'em,' he murmured, peering intently through a dusty pane. 'They shift like flies.'

'Dung flies,' added the storekeeper cynically. He craned for a better view. 'What they plannin'? They goin' to hit us now? Or mebbe they'll wait for the others to ride in.' He lapsed into thought for a moment. 'What's the bettin' on them scum catchin' up with the fella in the sands?'

'I wouldn't bet on anythin' concernin' him,' said Doc. 'In fact–'

But that was as far as he got before the crack of a single shot was followed by the snap of Mitchell's voice from somewhere in the shadows across the street.

'I ain't for understandin' what you townsfolk are about,' he began in an almost dismissive tone, 'but it sure looks one hundred per cent mule-headed from here. You ain't goin' to change nothin', not no how, in no way, so you might just as well finish the effort here and now.'

He waited, spat, creaked a couple of

156

footfalls across the boardwalk planking. 'I'll give you 'til nightfall. That'll be just short of another hour, then you all troop out of there like good citizens and we'll let bygones be bygones. And if it is that you're all armed – which I'm sure you are, thanks to the blind stupidity of Sheriff Prinz – don't figure for you havin' an edge there. You ain't nothin' like got an edge. I'll show you!'

Gunfire spat and blazed from all angles; left, right, high and low, searing into the timbers of the saloon like flaming irons. Windows splintered, slivers of glass and wood flew across the bar. The girls screamed and huddled in a heap on the floor. Bottles fell to pieces where they stood. Glasses shattered to a thousand shards; tables and chairs overturned and were scattered in the sudden mayhem as town men dived for cover or tried vainly to return the fire at targets they could not see and had no hope of finding.

. Elmer Puce had pulled his hat tight down over his face in an effort to shut out the noise. Tinker Johnny was at a window shooting wildly into the street, mouthing curses with every shot. Picky Layton was sweating, glancing nervously at the heap of girls, worrying that somewhere in the chaos there was a bullet destined for him. George Wickham and Hank Stone stood either side of the batwings, taking it in turns to fire a volley of shots more in anger than hope of ever hitting anything.

Doc moved among the town men, dressing flesh where he could, reassuring the nervous. Shamrock followed in his shadow. She tapped him on the shoulder and indicated a sprawled body to her left. 'There,' she mouthed. Doc nodded and crawled to the man's side.

Mopps went on all fours behind the bar, murmuring over and over that he would never get the place clean again. Ma McCundrie creaked her wheelchair from one patch of deep shadow to the next, the Colt tight in her grip, her head spinning with thoughts of how much all this was costing. Soon there would be nothing standing, not a thing remaining whole. Well, somebody would have to pay. You bet.

The gunfire died as a glowing lantern shattered and the bar was plunged into darkness.

CHAPTER TWENTY-ONE

'Another attack like that, and we'll be done.' George Wickham took a swig from a newly opened bottle of whiskey and offered the bottle to Doc.

'Not yet,' said Doc, tightening his rolled-up sleeves. 'There's men need lookin' to.'

Wickham closed his eyes. 'Hell, and that was only a half of Mitchell's force. Wait 'til them fellas get back from the sands.'

'We'll be ready.' Tinker Johnny grinned, spinning the chamber of his freshly loaded Colt. 'Won't be so easy for them scum next time.'

The storekeeper opened his eyes and sniffed deeply. 'Goddamn it, you can smell death even now. How many we lost?'

'Tommy Barr's dead,' said Hank Stone, still keeping watch on the street from the batwings. 'Chem Lucas don't look so good. Be a miracle if he lives. The rest is just cuts, scratches, bruises – and shock. It's the shock that did it. And now they're gettin' worried. Suppose Mitchell turns on the women and young 'uns. If that happens–'

'But he ain't, not yet,' said Tinker. 'So let's not reckon on the worst. We've got to get busy here.'

Shamrock hissed for Doc to join her at the side of a man with a head wound. Picky Layton slid away from the bar's darkened windows to join Wickham and Tinker. Mopps busied himself with a besom, pan and dustpan behind the bar. Ma creaked her chair to the glow of a newly lit lantern and invited the men to help themselves to drinks. She still had the Colt in her grip.

'I'm goin' out there,' said Tinker Johnny, fixing his Colt in his belt. 'Somebody's got to. We need a closer eye on Mitchell and what he's doin'. I'm volunteerin'.'

'I'll come with you,' offered Hank, already checking over his Colt.

Tinker laid a hand on the livery-owner's arm. 'No, Hank, this is a job for one man workin' things his own way. Two of us might get spotted. I stand a better chance by my-self. But thanks, anyhow.'

Hank nodded and holstered his gun. Wickham gestured from the window. 'Night's closin' tighter. Street's deserted. Now might be your best chance.'

'Still nothin' of the men Mitchell sent to

the sands,' murmured Wickham, pressing his face as close as he dare to the window. 'Goddamnit, you don't suppose–'

'There ain't no virtue nor salvation in supposin', George Wickham,' snapped Ma above the restless creaks of her wheelchair. She spun her Colt clumsily between gnarled, toad fingers. 'Leastways, not around here there ain't. Best let Tinker get on with what he's reckonin' before he changes his mind.' She eyed the man as if about to swat him. 'Use the back way. Stay in the shadows and off the street. See and hear what you can, then get back here smartish. No messin'.'

'You got it, Ma,' said Tinker through a half-grin. 'See you later.'

The others watched him go. A town girl blew him a kiss. Mopps silenced his besom and poured himself a drink. 'And good luck to you, Tinker Johnny.' He smiled, raising the glass.

The wheelchair creaked ominously. 'T'ain't luck he needs,' muttered Ma. 'It's prayers.'

Evening had passed, the long afternoon shadows merged to bring the night down suddenly, as if in a blink, thought Tinker, closing the back door to the saloon quietly behind him.

He waited, watching, listening. Nothing moved, there were no sounds, not even the howl of a night dog. He swallowed, conscious of a dry throat, the sweat beginning to bead on his brow, his clammy hands. Maybe this was not such a good idea. Maybe he should have accepted Hank's offer. It would have been safer.

He moved quickly from cover to cover; from behind a barrel, a broken crate, to the side of a disused shed, a half-open door on rusted hinges, always closing on the blaze of light ahead at the sheriff's office. How close should he get? Close enough to hear voices, make out what was being said? He needed to know what Mitchell was planning; what he intended in his next move. The town had to be ready. Everybody had to be ready.

He pushed on, cursing when he tripped, knocked a crate aside but halted it inches from the ground. He cleared the sweat from his face, tightened his gaze on the office. There was a side window. If he could reach that...

He was there in less than a minute. He took a deep breath, gathered himself and pressed an ear to the clapboard. Voices, a low, soft hum of sound, but nothing he could decipher clearly. He could recognize Mitchell, though; there was no mistaking his tone, and he was having plenty to say judging by the steady drone. Giving out orders, no doubt, plotting how he would reduce the saloon to a heap of rubble. If only he could hear...

He turned sharply at the new sounds and flattened his back to the boards. What in the name of...? Horses, riders, tack jangling, leather creaking. A sudden cloud of dust. Mitchell's men!

Tinker slid clear of the office wall, across a patch of open alleyway to a spot behind a buckboard from where he had a view of the street and the pool of light that poured like a freak sun as the door to the office swung open and Mitchell and his sidekicks crowded the boardwalk.

He counted the riders: two, three, four, five... 'Five?' he murmured to himself. 'Only five,' he repeated, blinking on a sudden surge of sweat across his eyebrows. 'Hell!' he hissed. He was certain a dozen men had ridden out. At least a dozen. He stiffened, the sweat chilling on his face, as Mitchell stepped forward from his men and addressed the riders.

'What happened?' he asked, his dark gaze

scanning the dusty, weary-eyed group still slumped exhausted in their saddles. 'You look as if you've ridden out of hell.'

'We have,' growled a black-haired man with a thickening salt-and-pepper stubble. He spat sand and wiped the back of his hand across his mouth. 'Hell – there ain't no other way of puttin' it.'

'He ambushed us soon as it got dark,' mumbled a man with a curled-back brim to his battered hat. 'Waited at an outcrop and shot us up as we came through. Seven of us. Will, Sam, Jamie, old Charlie...'

'Who shot you up, f'crissake?' growled Mitchell again.

'Whoever's out there, that's who,' spat a rider angrily. 'Same fella who was givin' Prinz all that trouble. He was right, there is somebody. And I for one ain't got a snitch of an idea who he is, savin' that he moves about like he was a ghost.'

The others murmured their agreement. 'That's it,' piped the black-haired man. 'A ghost. Fella's a ghost, and he's sure as hell intent on hauntin' us. Took us out just like that.' The man clicked his fingers. 'Thought nothin' of it. Nothin'. And he knew who we were. Oh, yes, he knew well enough. He was there like he was waitin' on us.'

'Did you get a sight of him?' asked Mitchell.

The man with the curled-back brim wiped a filthy bandanna over his face. 'Nothin'. Only his shadow. He was there behind his spittin' gunfire, then gone. Just disappeared into them sands as if they'd swallowed him.'

'Question is,' said another man among the riders, 'what are we goin' to do about him before he sets about us again? That's what we've gotta decide.'

The men murmured among themselves as they slid from their saddles and dusted themselves down. Mitchell's eyes burned like coals. A man at his side whispered in his ear.

'Mebbe we should quit this town right now,' piped a man on the boardwalk. 'Ride out for the border soon as it's light. We could be clear through in a day. Two at most.'

'There'll be no ridin' out,' snapped Mitchell. 'Time ain't right and we aren't ready. We stay like we planned. This town is ours whatever happens.' He turned his gaze on the saloon. 'Just in need of some cleanin' up, that's all. And we'll get to that at sunup.' He grinned cynically. 'Yeah, that's it, a clean sweep at dawn...'

Tinker Johnny swallowed, blinked and for

a moment felt a shiver rattle his bones. He had seen enough and heard enough. Time to move.

Minutes later he was back among the discarded crates and empty barrels.

CHAPTER TWENTY-TWO

Tinker Johnny's account of the events he had witnessed that night did nothing to ease the tension or calm the fears of the towns-folk gathered in the saloon. They heard him out in a stiff silence where no one moved, shifted a foot or so much as raised a glass to parched lips. There was an intake of breath, the scrape of a chair when Tinker came to tell of the riders who had returned from the sands. 'Just five, I swear to it,' he said quietly. 'Counted them – twice.'

The silence settled, this time stunned and amazed. An old-timer wheezed on his pipe. 'Some shootin', eh, if the fella out there downed seven of the rats. Now that is shootin'.'

'He used the night to his advantage,' reflected Doc. 'Knew where to be at just the right time. Be as easy as shootin' toads in a bucket to a fella like him.'

'Yeah, as you say: *like him, but who is he?*' Hank Stone frowned. 'We still don't know.'

'Just be grateful he's around, eh?' piped the old-timer behind a cloud of smoke.

The men agreed. The bar-girls chattered like fledglings. Shamrock shushed them. Ma McCundrie wheeled herself to the bar where Mopps poured brandy from her personal bottle. 'Here's to him, whoever he is,' she growled, raising her glass. The gathering joined her.

'Hold it,' counselled Elmer Puce, adjusting his hat. 'Let's not forget them that's died here today. And let's remind ourselves that we ain't got nothin' to toast yet.' He gazed reverentially over the attentive faces. 'What's Mitchell goin' to do now? Think on that. How's he goin' to seek his retribution? And mark my words, he will. You can bet to it.'

'Elmer's right,' said Doc, stepping to the centre of the room. 'Mitchell ain't goin' to risk sendin' men back to the sands, but he ain't goin' to sit it out waitin' on the stranger ridin' in. No, he'll be doin' just as Tinker's reported to us: he'll be havin' his so-called "clean sweep". And that means us plumb in the firin' line.'

'How long can we hold out?' asked Picky bluntly.

'An hour at best – if we get lucky,' came a voice from a shadowed corner.

'Bah!' scowled Ma, spinning her wheel-chair from the bar. 'That's yellowneck talk. We'll have none of it, you hear?'

'But it's mebbe fact, Ma,' said Tinker lighting a cheroot. 'Way Mitchell was lookin' last I saw of him, I wouldn't put nothin' past him. He wants Mission Rock. He plans holin' up here awhiles, and there ain't goin' to be nothin' stoppin' him. We can mebbe fight from here, but, hell, for how long is goin' to be anybody's guess. And if he gets to holdin' the women and young 'uns hostage, then we're done for anyhow.' He blew a thin line of smoke to the lantern's soft glow. 'But I'll fight, make no mistake.'

The men talked and murmured among themselves. Some found comfort and sup-port in tobacco; some turned to whiskey; some to both. Mopps completed his clean-up and viewed his efforts with satisfaction. Doc went back to the wounded. Ma gulped brandy and scowled. The bar girls broke from their huddled clutch and moved freely among the town men.

It was Shamrock who broke the atmosphere of unease and uncertainty. 'Mission Rock ain't goin' to be of no use to Mitchell and his boys if it ain't here, is it?'

Her words fell across the bar as if a handful of rocks had been tossed through the batwings. The talk and murmurings died. Ma's face cleared. The bar girls halted where they stood. A freckle-faced, bright-eyed girl sank thankfully to a waiting lap. Gazes turned on Shamrock.

'What sort of talk is that, Shamrock?' asked a lone voice huskily. 'What you sayin' there?'

Pairs of eyes followed her like lights as she came into the full glow of the lantern. She was a fine figure of a woman, still in her prime, with a mind as sharp as a blade and a determination that gleamed in her steady gaze. She smiled faintly, ran a finger over a still dark bruise in her neck – a painful reminder of Denes – and leaned forward, her hands flat on the table in front of her.

'We ain't come this far just to give up without a fight,' she began. 'We've got guns, true enough, but mebbe we would be out-gunned by Mitchell and his boys. They're professional. We ain't nothin' like professional.' The men murmured. Shamrock waited for silence before going on: 'But we do have an edge. Only one, but it is an edge, and it's ours.'

'And what might that be, ma'am?' asked the old-timer as a cloud of smoke cleared the top of his hat.

Shamrock's gaze hardened. 'The town,' she said. 'We have the town. We know it, every last plank and scratch of dirt of it. Damnit, some of us here helped build the place.' The men murmured and nodded again. The old-timer released more smoke. 'And we know exactly how to destroy it.'

'Destroy it?' came a bevy of voices at once.

'That's what I said,' called Shamrock above the clamour. 'And that's what I mean.' She stood fully upright at the table.

Ma banged her brandy-glass on the arm of her wheelchair. 'Hear the lady out, damn you!' she demanded. 'Show a bit of respect there.'

The voices fell silent. Eyes went back to Shamrock.

'Here's my plan,' she began again. 'We start a fire – two fires for preference, three if we can manage it. We put all the old out-buildings, shacks and sheds back of the main street to the torch. We work in parties of four, five, a half-dozen at most. The fires begin at more or less the same time. Result, confusion. Mitchell and his boys won't know what's burnin' because they don't know the lay-out of the town like we do.'

'That's makin' sense so far,' said Hank as Doc Cherry nodded and the men's attention focused on Shamrock. 'Then what?'

'I'm figurin' on Mitchell's men bein' disorganized,' said Shamrock, leaning forward again on the table. 'He'll scatter them in an attempt to put out the fires, and that's when we step in. We'll be waitin'. And we won't be tight as nuts in winter in one building. We'll be here, there, anywhere where there's a Mitchell man in target.' She paused a moment. 'We move an hour before sun-up. What do you reckon?'

There was very little reckoning to be done. It took only minutes for the town men to be agreed that Shamrock's plan was workable – and, more important, a better wage than remaining holed up in the saloon.

'We'll take our chance out there,' said one, summing up the general mood. 'If we can get Mitchell and his sidekicks figurin' what to do it'll be worth it. One thing's for sure, he'll have a helluva lot of cleanin' up to do!'

Elmer Puce and Picky Layton along of the

old-timer volunteered to stand to Ma, the bar-girls and Mopps. They could not be left to fend for themselves in spite of Ma's protestations and her vow that any Mitchell critter steppin' within six feet of her would be spillin' his guts in seconds.

A half-hour later the men had broken into four groups – the 'torch gangs' as they dubbed themselves – and were planning their separate strategies.

Doc had taken Shamrock aside. 'I ain't happy about you bein' in on all this, 'specially not out there. You ain't fully recovered yet. Mebbe it'd be better if you stayed back here with Ma and the girls.'

Shamrock had smiled and laid an affectionate hand on Doc's arm. 'Appreciate your concern, Doc, but I wouldn't miss this for the world.' The smile faded. 'Can't help thinkin', though, what that fella out there in the sands is doin'. Do you reckon for him still bein' there, or has he left? Mebbe he's gone to raise help. What do you figure?'

Doc did not figure anything where the stranger was concerned. How could he? The man was his own law and maybe his own destiny.

The first flames, fanned on the soft morning

breeze behind Wickham's mercantile, licked at the dawn skies as a flicker of light broke in the east. Five minutes later a larger, fiercer fire took hold in the old barn at the rear of Hank Stone's livery. A third followed behind the barber's, and a fourth, in a blaze of mocking defiance, at the back of the sheriff's office.

And the doors of hell opened.

CHAPTER TWENTY-THREE

Mayhem erupted with shouts, yells, barked orders that no one heeded; tumbling, stumbling bodies as Mitchell's men poured through the door of the sheriffs office like a tide of human lava. They found their feet on the boardwalk, some spreading to the street, one still clutching a half-empty bottle, another hitching his pants frantically, and stared into the flame-lit sky, their mouths hanging open in a state of disbelief.

'Well, don't just stand there, do somethin', damn you!' cursed Mitchell, grabbing a man by the shoulder. 'You get back in there and guard them moneybags with your life.

You hear me? Your life. And don't leave em, not for nothin'.' He grabbed hold of another man. 'You help him. Goddamnit, there's a fortune back there. Shift!'

'Four separate fires, boss,' yelled a man in the middle of the street.

'I've got eyes,' snapped Mitchell. 'I can see 'em.'

The men began to fan out in small groups. One group headed for the fire at the livery, another for the blaze behind the store. Four men ran, bent low, their faces already lathered with sweat, towards Picky Layton's barber's shop.

Some men still stood in the Street as if in a trance at the sight of the flames as they danced and swayed and leapt ever higher.

'Sonofabitch, the whole place'll go up,' mouthed a dark-eyed man with a moth-eaten stubble that glistened with sweat.

'Somebody go look to the horses, fcris'sake. Get 'em clear,' shouted an older man with a shock of grey hair that reached to his shoulders.

Mitchell seethed and spat his curses as he watched his men scatter. His eyes narrowed. Every town man living would pay for this, he vowed. He would kill them all, every last one. And maybe the women too. His gaze settled on the saloon. And he would begin right there, he thought, motioning for one of his men to join him. The bar-girls and that toad of an old woman trundling round in her wheelchair. But he would spare just one girl. Just one. For personal reasons.

He growled and ordered the sidekick to follow him.

'It's gettin' out of hand,' shouted George Wickham above the crack and spit of flames, the crumbling collapse of timbers and showering sparks.

Doc Cherry ducked instinctively at the sudden blaze of shooting that seemed to break all round him. He nodded at the storekeeper and indicated they should seek deeper cover.

'Where's Mitchell?' asked Wickham when they were into the safety of the small porch at the back of the store. 'You seen anythin' of him?'

'Nothin',' said Doc, wiping his eyes against the smart of smoke and thickening air. 'But you can bet he'll be plannin' somethin' grisly. It's in his nature.'

They watched the flames for a moment before another blaze of shots, indecipherable yells and shouts and the whinnying of horses stirred Doc into stepping clear of the porch. 'Time I did my rounds, so to speak,' he said, settling his hat and covering his mouth with a bandanna.

'I'm right with you, Doc,' said Wickham, nodding. 'I'll work my way to the livery first, see how Hank's gettin' on. Then I'll head back to the saloon. Ma and the gals ain't got a deal of protection.'

Doc raised a hand in acknowledgement and disappeared into the swirl of smoke. Wickham followed, setting a fast pace in the opposite direction. Neither had noticed the darker shape of the man silhouetted against the backdrop of swaying flames. He had merely smiled quietly to himself, reloaded his rifle and melted away.

A dead man lay at Tinker Johnny's feet. A town youth, barely mid-teens, with a ruddy glow to his spotty face, stared wild-eyed into the smoke and flames. 'I been hit, Tinker,' he gasped, clamping a hand to his upper arm. 'Goddamnit, I'm bleedin'! You see this, Tinker? You see what I got?'

'I see,' said Tinker, 'but I'll sure as hell be lookin' at another dead man if you don't get your head down! Just get down, will you? Bind that arm best you can for now. Doc'll look to it later.'

Gunfire spat and cracked above their heads, kicked dust and thudded into the clapboard of the building at their backs. Tinker squinted into the smoke, flames and brightening light of the new day. Hell, he thought, if only he could see how many he had ranged against him. Three, four, a half-dozen? He had no idea, but however many they sure could shoot! Another hail of lead crashed around him. Much more of this and he would be a body in the dirt, the wounded youth along of him. Maybe he should move, take the youth with him.

They could make a dash for the far side of the street.

But Tinker did not move. He could not. He was too engrossed in the sounds, the spits, roars and blaze of a rifle being fired at a fast rate from somewhere in the shadows. All he could make out was the flame of the shots, the soft curls of smoke, and then the sudden silence of the guns that only seconds ago had threatened to destroy him.

'You hear that, Tinker?' hissed the youth, shuffling to his side. 'Hear that shootin'? That ain't one of the Mitchell gang. Not nohow it ain't.' The youth watched the blood trickling through his fingers as he gripped the wound. 'So who is it, Tinker? Who's doin' all that shootin'?'

'No idea, son, but I'm sure as hell grateful he's on our side!'

'We're losin' this, Hank,' said Wickham, ducking lower into the scant cover of straw-bales and a broken crate at the side of the forge. 'Mitchell's scum are gettin' the upper hand again. And if we ain't awful careful these fires are goin' to get bigger than we can handle.'

Hank Stone wiped a hand across his smarting eyes and motioned for the store-keeper to stay silent. He turned his gaze down the long stretch of the Street to the clutter of buildings wreathed in smoke and still dancing flames. 'You hear that?' he asked. 'Hear them shots?'

Wickham grunted, winced against the sudden crack and groan of collapsing timbers and turned his own gaze to follow the blacksmith's. 'Winchester,' he murmured. 'High-powered. Rapid shootin'. Real rapid.' He switched his gaze to Stone's face. 'That ain't Mitchell's lot.'

'Too right it ain't,' said Hank. 'I figure we've got a visitor...'

Ma McCundrie's eyes were as fierce and

bright as the fires licking through the old buildings across the street. She glared at Mitchell, then at the huddle of bar-girls in the far corner, at Mopps, wide-eyed and open-mouthed at the bar, flanked by Picky Layton and Elmer Puce; at Shamrock standing defiantly to the side of the 'wings. But she winked at Doc Cherry.

'I'll say it one more time so's you'll fully understand,' growled Mitchell, pacing across the bar, disregarding the gunfire in the street, the yelling, shouting and creaking timbers. He halted, glanced at the faces watching him. 'I want an end to this madness out there. Now! Immediately. And if an end ain't forthcomin', then me and my partner here' – he gestured to the sidekick watching from the shadows – 'him and me will start killin' you off. One by one. Some quick, some not so quick. Understand? 'Course you do. So you, Shamrock, will get out there on the boardwalk and start shoutin' out the deal. They'll get to listenin' when they see it's you. But if they don't...'

Doc sweated and seethed quietly, but his deeper attention was elsewhere. He was listening to the gunfire beyond the bar. The crack and spit of Colts ahead of bursts of rifle shots, and just occasionally rapid firing, faster than he had ever heard in Mission Rock or anywhere else come to that. A rifle in the hands of someone who meant a whole lot more than just everyday business. This fellow meant deadly, vengeful business. Had it escaped Mitchell, he wondered?

'Let's get started,' ordered Mitchell, grabbing Shamrock's arm and dragging her to the 'wings.

'I'll see you in hell if anythin' happens to her,' spat Ma, flicking her gaze to the guns taken from those who had remained in the saloon and guarded now by the gang leader's sidekick.

'Don't doubt it for one minute,' sneered Mitchell, his parched, cracked lips sliding to a twisted grin.

Doc stiffened. Picky took a half-step forward, but was restrained by the undertaker with a shake of his head; Shamrock stumbled under the grip on her arm and tossed her hair angrily.

'There's too much noise and confusion out there,' cried Doc in an effort to stall Mitchell. 'She can shout all she likes, but she ain't goin' to be heard. You're wastin' your time.'

Mitchell scowled and tightened his grip on Shamrock's arm. 'Save it, Doc. This is my show and I'll do—'

Picky's patience snapped as he pulled clear of Elmer and flung himself at Mitchell. The sidekick's gun roared, filling the bar with thudding sound. Picky cursed, lost his balance, grabbed at his thigh already spouting blood, and hit the floor in a scrambling heap.

Mitchell glared, spat and grinned. 'Let him watch himself bleedin', then finish him.' He nodded to the sidekick.

A bar-girl stifled a scream, another sobbed. Ma spun her wheelchair. Mopps swallowed. Doc had reached for his bag when the 'wings burst open and a tall dark figure in a long dustcoat stood silhouetted against the morning light, the gleaming barrel of a rifle steady and ranged ahead of him.

He fired a single shot to throw the sidekick clean across the bar.

CHAPTER TWENTY-FOUR

There was a fixed, unnatural stillness in the seconds that followed. The shot echo soared and was lost; the bar-girls clung together like a ball of colourful moths; Mitchell stared; Shamrock had fallen to her knees, and Ma's wheelchair stayed hauntingly silent.

It was Doc who made the first move, disregarding the silhouetted shape at the 'wings as he gave only a cursory glance at the dead sidekick and settled at Picky Layton's side where Elmer was already comforting the fellow best he knew how.

Shamrock watched as the man's gun barrel ranged an unmoving aim on Rogan Mitchell's gut. 'Best clear yourself of weapons, mister,' said the man in a flat, dry tone. 'I ain't for wastin' lead unnecessarily, but I will, I surely will, if provoked. Weapons. Now.'

Mitchell unbuckled his gun belt and let it drop to the floor with a thud. 'You've been sittin' on my tail for a whole sight longer than's healthy, fella,' he drawled, his eyes working frantically for some activity out in the street. 'And, frankly, I'm tired of it, so I welcome this chance to meet you head on – for the short time it's likely to be.' A sneering grin broke and faded. Mitchell's face clouded and grew ashen. 'But just who the hell are you?'

The man did not move. The light behind him flickered through long, contorted shadows. 'The past,' he said at last in that same flat tone.

Ma's wheelchair creaked. Shamrock's hair gleamed wet under her sweat. She blinked, licked her lips, came fully upright and eased away from Mitchell. Mopps's hand moved automatically to a glasscloth which he gripped as if having taken hold of a safe, secure hand. The man in the 'wings watched every movement, missed nothing; listened, it seemed to Ma, for every next breath.

'The past, eh?' sneered Mitchell, his eyes still working, darting to left and right, from the body of his sidekick to the guns he had taken and his own belt at his feet. 'Well, now, that spans an awful big time, mister, and I'd sure–'

'The Berristone raid,' began the man, his tone as dry as the ash gathering in the fire-scorched shacks and barns behind him. 'The killin's at Candy Rock; murder and robbery at Fulsome; the rape and murder at the Carrington spread; shootin' up of the sheriff and his men at Blenheim; bank-robbery at Sweetfields; massacre at San Mendos; more rape and pillage at Condice; the dead men, women and children at Northforks...'

The sweat beaded like driven rain on Mitchell's face. No one moved; no one

183

breathed a sound. No one, it seemed, drew breath.

For the first time the man's eyes gleamed. 'You personally ravaged Mae Cunningham and then cut her throat; you shot Joel Kindling in the back; raped and strangled the Sanderson sisters – they were just twelve years old; you ordered the hangin' of Charlie Betters, Mick McCoon and Henry Leigh out Penistock way; you shot Jamie Brown because he defended his daughter against your lust, then you shot her; you buried alive the manager of the bank at Fieldstock. It was you, Rogan Mitchell, who–'

'Enough!' yelled Ma, creaking her wheelchair into painful life. 'We've heard enough, I say. Whoever you are, mister, take him. Take the rat, the scumbag, two-bit louse and do your worst!'

'You bet, your very worst,' murmured Picky.

'Do it, mister,' echoed Mopps.

Doc patted Picky's arm and stood up, for the first time conscious of a new sound, or no sound at all, he thought, a frown deepening like a trough across his wet brow. The gunfire had ceased, the voices had fallen away to no more than the occasional shout. He recognized the voices: town men. So what, he wondered.

'Your men are scatterin', Mitchell,' said the man. 'They're desertin' you. They're scared. And there's no money.'

Mitchell made to move but froze again under the jerked probe of the rifle barrel.

'The town men have won back their homes,' the man continued, the tone of his voice still steady. 'Mission Rock is theirs again – includin' the sheriff's office. Ain't that where you were holdin' the Northforks raid money? I understand so.' The rifle moved fractionally. 'Pity. Looks to me like you've lost it.

Saliva dribbled at the corner of Mitchell's mouth.

'Tell me who you are, mister. Tell me,' he croaked, 'and I'll see you in damnation...'

Mitchell's lunge for the weapons his sidekick had collected was fast but clumsy. He reached, felt his fingers on the butt of a Colt, gripped it and had the gun steadied in an aim on the target of the silhouetted shape when the rifle roared.

A bar-girl screamed. Ma spun the wheelchair through a half-circle. Mopps ducked behind the bar. Elmer Puce fell across Picky Layton's legs. Doc lowered himself in a bizarre state of slow motion behind a table, weariness clouding his expression. Shamrock crawled to his side and watched Mitchell stumble, drop the Colt, grasp his gut and roll his eyes at the faceless shape in the 'wings.

Those gathered in Ma McCundrie's saloon bar that day were of one mind in the detail of the final moments of Rogan Mitchell's death. He died, they said, with five words crawling like lice from his mouth:

'Who the hell are you?'

'And now we ain't goin' to know, are we? Leastways, that's how I'm seein' it.' Picky Layton winced, raised himself with the aid of a stick from the bench on the front veranda of McCundrie's bar and hobbled into the full glare of the sun.

He gazed down the dusty stretch of the street. 'Comin' on, ain't it? Another few weeks and no one would ever know that half this town went up in smoke. Pity the stranger ain't goin' to be here to see it.' He turned to face the others. 'And I guess he never will. He won't be back.'

'Can't say that for certain,' said Wickham, lighting a fresh cheroot. He blew a line of smoke to the high blue sky. 'You all heard what that Marshal Anderson out of North-forks reckoned. He said as how it was a known fact that the fella had been trailin' the Mitchell outfit for months just waitin' on the moment to strike. And Mission Rock was that moment, thank the Lord.'

'Amen to that.' Elmer Puce nodded, easing his hat from the gathering sweat on his head. 'Northforks was Mitchell's undoin', one raid too many. And he did himself no favours in recruitin' that scumbag Prinz.' He settled the hat again. 'Still, that don't tell us nothin' about the stranger. My own figurin' would be that Mitchell had at some time harmed him, mebbe killed a relative or somebody close, and the fella had vowed retribution no matter how long it took, no matter where the trail led and finally ended. Well, he sure had sweet revenge. Mitchell died like a cornered rat.'

'Sure he did,' said Tinker Johnny from the far end of the shadowed bench, 'but at one helluva price to Mission Rock. Evidence is all around ... on Boot Hill, in the ashes, the charred timbers out there. Oh, sure, it'll come together again; it's got to, it's where we are, where we belong. There'll be new faces, new lives, new talk, but I for one shan't be forgettin' what happened here.'

'Nobody will,' grunted Ma McCundrie, creaking her wheelchair expertly through the 'wings. 'Nobody will want to. We lived it – and so did the stranger. Me, I'll recall him for what he said he was: the past. And he was. Like the past, he caught up with Mitchell. So remember that; we've all got a past. We've all got a stranger out there in the sands.' Ma's face creased in one of her rare smiles. 'I see Hank Stone approachin'. He'll be for quenchin' his thirst. Let's join him, eh? On the house!'

In her softly shadowed room above the bar, Shamrock turned from the window and smiled at Doc Cherry. 'Funny, ain't it: a month ago I vowed, hand on the Good Book, that if I survived this hell of a town, I'd leave it fast as I could. Now, I don't want to. I couldn't.'

'Well, I'm sure pleased to hear that.' Doc grinned. 'Place wouldn't be the same without you.' He rolled his hat through his fingers. 'And neither would I come to that,' he added, without lifting his gaze.

Shamrock was silent for a moment. 'Same goes for me,' she said quietly. 'I guess ... what I mean is...' She tossed her hair and stiffened. 'Goddamnit, Doc, why don't you and me hitch ourselves legal while we've still got the time?'

'You mean, get wed?' gulped Doc.

'I mean just that.' Shamrock smiled.

'Well, I don't know to that, my dear. I'm gettin' old and you're still–'

'You doin' anythin' Saturday?' snapped Shamrock.

'Well, not that I know of.'

'Good. That'll be our weddin' day. Give this town somethin' to *really* talk about, eh?'

This Large Print Book, for people
who cannot read normal print,
is published under the auspices of

THE ULVERSCROFT FOUNDATION

... we hope you have enjoyed this book.
Please think for a moment about those
who have worse eyesight than you ...
and are unable to even read or enjoy
Large Print without great difficulty.

You can help them by sending a
donation, large or small, to:

**The Ulverscroft Foundation,
1, The Green, Bradgate Road,
Anstey, Leicestershire, LE7 7FU,
England.**
or request a copy of our brochure for
more details.

The Foundation will use all donations
to assist those people who are visually
impaired and need special attention
with medical research, diagnosis
and treatment.

Thank you very much for your help.